THE HEALING OF LUTHER GROVE

Barry Gornell

FREIGHT BOOKS

First published in the UK October 2012
By Freight Books
49-53 Virginia Street
Glasgow, G1 1TS
www.freightbooks.co.uk

A CIP catalogue reference for this book is available from the British Library
ISBN 978-1-908754-02-8

Typeset by Freight in Plantin

Printed and bound by Bell and Bain, Glasgow

the publisher acknowledges investment from
Creative Scotland toward the publication of this book

This book is dedicated to Carole

Barry Gornell was born in Liverpool and now lives on the West Coast of Scotland, trying to grow up with his children. He is supported by his wife. He is a novelist/screenwriter, ex fire-fighter, truck driver and book shop manager. His short films *Sonny's Pride* and *The Race* were broadcast on STV. Graduating from the University of Glasgow Creative Writing Masters programme in 2008, he was awarded a Scottish Book Trust New Writers Bursary in 2009. His short fiction has been published in *The Herald* newspaper, *Let's Pretend, 37 stories about (in)fidelity*, *Gutter 03* and *Gutter 04*. *The Healing of Luther Grove* is his first novel.

Luther Grove was content with four kills. Three had taken a bullet between the eye and the ear and dropped instantly; the fourth had spun in the air, dead before landing. The final headshot had dispatched an amorous male who'd been seeking to procreate with his recently deceased mate. The instant Luther got to his feet, the lucky ones had vanished underground. When he emerged from the overgrowth that concealed him, he shouldered his .22. He strode the twenty-five yards or so into the glade, to where the bodies lay. After expressing the remaining urine from each, he gutted them in the field, before the flesh had a chance to taint, collecting the edible organs in an airtight container. His game-bag full, he turned for home, aware of the crows, biding their time on the lower boughs.

Up until now, the ache had been constant yet bearable, something he carried with him. But as Luther entered the pines, an unexpected pang robbed him of his breath and creased him over. He slumped to his knees on the dry needle floor, using his rifle for support as his grip tightened around the stock. As he stifled a groan, it struck him that lying flat and still in the pre-dawn chill probably did little to help, although he knew the pain was unrelated to the cold. It gradually eased, his breathing stabilised, his heartbeat slowed and his muscles relaxed, allowing him to stand. He used his arm to wipe the cold sweat from his face.

When he stepped out from the tree-line, lower down the mountain, the dew had evaporated and the sun warmed his back.

Luther used a cleaver to remove each foot at the joint. The separation exposed a clean, rounded knuckle of bone either side of the blade. He turned the paunched rabbit onto its back. Starting at the left side of the cavity, he separated the gut muscle from the skin in much the same way he would open the pages of a book or magazine. Inserting his hand, he worked it around the spine to the other side until he cradled the pink torso in his four fingers. Holding the stripped chest with his left hand he peeled the skin over the back legs as though taking off the animal's socks, before working each front leg out of its fur. The effort of pulling the released skin forward and over the shoulders lifted the animal from the wooden board, exposing its neck. A neat purple hole showed where the single bullet had entered at the base of the skull: the stray shot that explained why this one had spun in the air. He was raising the cleaver to chop through the neck when he heard the growl of a diesel engine.

Through the window he could see a large red pickup coming down the track from the main road, tunnelling through the trees. It rolled with the ruts and potholes, puffing up summer dust clouds that hung in the morning glow like camouflage in the air. It stopped outside the new entrance to the Macpherson place. It wasn't the one that had stopped outside the old entrance, just over a year ago, or returned, two or three times in the intervening months. Nevertheless, this year's model, top of the range, shiny and over-equipped; it carried the same personalised registration plate, P4YNE.

Their arrival was imminent.

As the past year had turned, Luther had witnessed the derelict building being partially demolished and then disguised, rebuilt: twice the size with lots of glass. From inside his single story cottage, he'd watched surveyors and architects stride around the building site in the rain, falling leaves sticking to their hard hats and fluorescent vests. Heavy plant had churned the grass as it dug extra foundations. Local builders had laid brick and levelled floors. Specialist tradesmen had arrived with the triple glazing, cedar cladding, the under-floor heating, the cast iron oven, the imported bathroom and the complex electrical system that would maintain the levels of practically everything within the new walls. Recent weeks had seen delivery of new sofas, beds and other large items. The placing of these had been supervised by Cargill, the local estate agent, a small town man who appeared to be acting as the project's general flunky. Luther had watched Cargill lurking about the house late at night when there was no reason for him to be there, reluctant to leave, diminished with envy.

As the Macpherson ruin had been developed into a family home, with all modern conveniences, the grounds were landscaped to impose an extended footprint of order right up to the new hit-and-miss wooden fence that defined the boundary of ownership. Their property was a statement.

It had been eighteen days since the joiners, painters and landscape gardeners had put the finishing touches to the renovation, cleaned up the site and left, taking their tools with them. During these eighteen days, the green shoots of mare's tail and ground elder had already broken through the alien cleanliness of the pale gravel driveway. The uniform stones formed a flat, lifeless thoroughfare that surrounded a perfect island of lawn. The only remaining tree on the property stood in the centre of this lawn. The others had been felled and their stumps ground away to allow more light through the glass roof of the extension.

Luther saw a change in the man who stepped from his vehicle. His confidence was unchallenged. Tall, well-built and dressed head to toe in this season's outdoor gear, he put on a display of exaggerated stretching, as though their journey had been arduous, before broadening his chest and planting his feet to consider his domain. Each time the man had visited the work in progress, parading around the site, not needed and increasingly unwelcome, he had tried to ask the right question, say the right thing, laughing too loudly, too easily. Superficially, he appeared to seek acceptance, to be one of the lads. But what had become obvious to Luther, studying him unnoticed, like a twitcher in a hide, was that it was important for this man to let everybody who toiled there know that he was the owner, the guy they worked for. He didn't want their friendship, he wanted their thanks. This trait was common to many incomers, who would often be confused when 'these people' didn't burst with gratitude at their contribution, a contribution that had rarely been asked for. This man had the aspirations of a laird. He rankled Luther and he had taken pleasure in each of the man's departures, enjoying the harsh comments and laughter of the labourers, clearly relieved to be rid of him, making greater progress in his absence.

His woman followed and stood next to him. The woman he had last seen as an imago of waterproofs, bundling a papoose, had fully emerged. Her hair hung in a loose ponytail that swayed as she shook her head.

Luther barely felt the blade slicing through the pad of his thumb.

They put their arms around each other as they stared at the Macpherson place, their place, nodding in approval. She giggled and put her hands over her face. He pulled her right into his chest and kissed her on the top of her head. She hugged him.

Luther bound his handkerchief around his wound and applied pressure to it as he watched her lean into the back of their truck and lift their child from her safety seat. Mother held daughter up close and pointed to the house, laughing at her as she mimicked with her own outstretched arm. She carried her to the new gate, where the child wriggled down, eager to be on the floor. As she slid through her mother's arms her white cotton dress rode up over chubby thighs and a heavy nappy. The little girl held on to the wooden cross-bars, bouncing herself, working her legs as she peeked through the spaces. Her mother lifted the catch and motioned for the little girl to help her push. The girl stood transfixed, swaying as the gate swung away from her, revealing a new world, a kingdom of organised space. Luther was surprised how much the child had grown. Although she still held onto her mother's hand, her steps were steady and she negotiated the gravel and the gradient with confidence. Her hair looked as though it had never been cut. Long golden wisps trapped the life of the sun as they left the shade of the trees that lined the lane.

The man started the engine, inched forward, tipped the front of the truck through the gateway and rolled down to the house, crunching his path through the gravel for the first time. The child waved as he passed them. The movement of her arm almost caused her to lose balance and only her mother's grip on her wrist kept her upright.

Luther used a twisting motion to dislocate the vertebrae and separate the rabbit's head from its body.

Laura Payne's hands were cupped over her mouth and nose as she gazed at the property in front of her. The last time she had been here it had still looked like a construction site, the bare bones of a home. Now here it was, delivered, complete. She couldn't believe this was their new home; their combined ideas and desires made real.

The house sat at an angle to the driveway, presenting a front door that was recessed into the corner, the overhang of which provided an open porch, it being part of the cedar-wood decking that formed a raised walkway around the three walls of glass and concrete, one solely of glass, that surrounded the remains of the original humble cottage.

When she looked at John, who stood beside her with Molly in his arms, she gave in and the sob that had been caught in her chest was released. Tears ran down her face. Molly didn't understand. Her face creased and reddened as she began to cry in sympathy with mummy, leaning across from daddy's arms. Laura laughed as she took Molly from John and tried to comfort her. But the laughter didn't reassure her; it only confused her even more, increasing the volume of her crying. Her mouth was as wide as it could be, her molars still breaking through the upper gum.

'Well,' said John Payne, 'I wasn't expecting this.'

'She's fine,' said Laura, wiping Molly's face. 'She just doesn't like to see her mummy cry, do you?' She kissed Molly and held her close, whispering into her ear. The baby put an arm around Laura's neck and fixed her mouth around her free thumb.

'She's tired?' said John. 'After sleeping all the way here?'

'Maybe. Just being up early, out of her routine I suppose.'

As Molly calmed herself, Laura listened to the birdsong and the sough of the wind in the pine forest that stretched for miles beyond their property. Reeds tipped their heads as one towards the dark water of the lochan that lay in the marshland between their house and the main road. Bees buzzed amongst the gorse growing along the edge of the lane as the incongruous scent of coconut floated through the air. A buzzard perched on a distant fence post, tearing at the kill it gripped in its talons.

'Do you think it looks out of place? Too modern?'

'Not at all,' said John, without thinking, 'it's beautiful.'

'I suppose people will get used to it, given time.'

'They do or they don't; it's here. And so are we: a new start.'

Laura's tummy fluttered at the phrase. The reason for it flooded through her.

'It is beautiful, isn't it?'

'And this is only the outside,' said John. 'Come on, open the door.'

'I haven't got the key.'

'It's not locked.'

John gestured for her to go first. Stepping onto the porch, Laura turned the brass handle and pushed. She let go. The door swept open like a welcoming arm, inviting them in.

'Well go on,' said John, ushering her in with a pat on the backside, 'I haven't seen it finished either.'

The first thing that struck her was the light. Sunshine bounced off pale walls and polished floors with such force that it appeared to be magnified, brighter inside the house than outside. It was warm. It was quiet. She could smell the freshness of the plaster, the paint and most of all the waxed sap of the specially imported American oak that was underfoot throughout. The oak was the only thing John had insisted upon, his one tantrum. He couldn't explain his need and never sought to reduce its significance as Laura had sat through the whole performance; a list of things he was happy to give her carte blanche with; kitchen and bathroom, layout, furniture and fittings, which rooms would be used for what, the colours they would be painted, what wouldn't be allowed in certain rooms, where the new furniture would go, what this furniture would be, sofas, chairs, tables, curtains, rugs, and on and on and on, down to the colour of their new towels or even if she wanted to change the toothpaste they had always used; he'd go along with it all, for this one concession on her part. She had thought it a significant gesture on his part and a small sacrifice for her to make at the time, but now she saw it dominated every room, made it one space, his space. She knew already that the floor would be exclaimed as the master stroke, the choice that unified the house, made it whole.

'Oh my,' said John, 'just look at that floor, the way that it catches the light. What did I say, babe, didn't I tell you?'

'You did,' she replied

'Okay, which way do you want to go?' he said.

They stood and considered their options.

The downstairs consisted of four connected, open plan rooms that ran like a circuit around the core of the house, the original building. The exterior walls of the Macpherson place had been retained, integrated in such a way that the single room created within what had been a two-roomed cottage now formed the calm heart of their project. The stonework had been cleaned up but left exposed; a rough and natural foil to the clean lines of the walls that now encased it.

To their left, the wall of glass of the sunroom afforded a southerly view across their lochan. A moorhen and her chick paddled through the reed-bed on the far shore, oblivious of their new neighbours.

The room to their right was more a broad passage. At the end, a spiral staircase climbed up to the bedrooms. Above this room a lattice of beams and rafters supported a glass walkway that allowed light from the upper level to permeate, dappling the ground floor with shadow.

'Let Molly decide,' said Laura.

She put Molly down and they watched. Molly looked at the vastness beyond the glass wall and almost staggered backwards, overwhelmed. Leaning on the glass, she grinned at her parents, unsure, her eyes still moist but now full of intrigue. Turning away from them, leaving handprints behind, she walked down the corridor, concentrating on the ground, stepping in and out of the broken patches of light, fascinated by her own shadow, uninterested in the doors that were being opened by John and Laura as they followed behind; cloakroom, utility room, downstairs toilet, laundry.

Molly ignored the spiral stairs and toddled around into a spacious dining area, dominated by the long beech table with seating for twelve that had come from John's boardroom. She walked along the length of the pale green room under the table. A strip of window echoed the dimensions of the tabletop, affording diners a clear view of the densely wooded mountain slopes of forestry land, beyond which lay the hidden village of Milton, the nearest population centre. Whilst allowing in more than enough light, the architect had claimed the proximity of the trees would help provide a sense of intimacy when the diners were seated. The deep surround, angled into the window like a horizontal archer's slit in a castle rampart, drew the eye outside and disallowed the presence of any domestic clutter in the frame.

The kitchen, the fourth side of the square, was to be Laura's playground. She looked in every cupboard, slid every drawer out on its silent casters to let them glide back in again, peeled the protective film from the surface of each appliance, clicked on the gas burners, the fan, the overheads, all the time getting giddier. John swivelled on one of the breakfast stools, grinning at Laura. Then they noticed Molly wasn't there.

'Molly.'

'She'll be under the table,' said John.

Laura stepped past him and checked.

'No, she's not. Oh shit,' said Laura, 'the stairs. I told you we should have taken the gate out of the pickup.'

'She won't have gone up the stairs, she's too small.'

Laura skipped up the staircase, a smile on her face, hoping she had made it this far after all.

'Molly, Molly, Molly.'

Natural light flooded the central corridor, which was glazed at both ends and ran beneath a glass ridge. The four bedroom doors were still closed. She quickly looked into each room, just in case.

John was waiting at the bottom of the stairs. He crooked his index finger a couple of times and turned away for her to follow.

When she walked into the sunroom, he was pointing at the door into the Macpherson place, also American oak. It was ajar. Laura tiptoed over and pushed. She stepped inside.

This room was darker than the rest of the house. The original window spaces, now double-glazed against sound, allowed light in from the surrounding rooms. The stone walls absorbed it. One gable end was lined with empty bookshelves, incorporating a low level wine rack. There was a club sofa and a matching armchair. Underfoot was a thick ruby carpet. Laura's feet sank into it. Molly lay sleeping in the middle of the room like a small white ghost. John and Laura closed the door behind them and sat down either side of their little girl.

'I guess she likes this room best,' said John.

'Mmm, can you blame her?' said Laura, her hand sinking into the pile. 'We should call it the snug. That okay with you?'

'Whatever.'

Looking around, Laura couldn't imagine how it would feel when the rest of their belongings arrived. This room didn't need anything else. Good people had soaked into the stone. 'I don't think there was any sadness within these walls.'

'It's haunted?'

'Benevolent spirits,' said Laura, 'no malice. It feels calm, don't you think, protective?'

'Like a womb?' said John, arching an eyebrow, 'Don't go all new age on me, start painting the walls with menstrual blood and looking for your female drum.'

'Shut up.' She was almost annoyed with him, but she knew he was uncertain. John's first response to most things was volume. But now, he was practically whispering. He could have been in church. 'You know what I mean. Not a womb, more of a grotto.'

'I'm sorry. I know what you mean. It's – it's not like the rest of the house.'

'It's the heart of the house.'

'No. She is.'

Laura stared at Molly, hurt but not surprised at being openly usurped.

'Not me?'

'Not since she came along.'

She could have brushed this off as daughter devotion but knew that wasn't it at all. No one to blame but myself, she thought.

Luther worked at the draining board most of the morning, scraping residual flecks of flesh and fat from the skins until they were clean enough to cure. Once stretched and tacked onto a board he covered them with a layer of salt, making sure he treated every bit of skin, teasing it into any folds. All the while he took note of what was unloaded from the removals van that had backed down to the new house not long after they had arrived. Less than he had expected; a small television, computer equipment, rails of clothes and boxes, some of which were taken straight to the kitchen, others, small and heavy enough to suggest books, were taken into the centre room, his favourite. The man helped the driver unload, talking and laughing loudly, taking pleasure in his own conversation. She unpacked their pickup, which contained all things baby. She brought drinks out when they had finished, tipped the driver before he left. Within an hour the van was climbing out of their driveway and the man and woman had closed the door, their arrival complete.

Pulling out of their driveway, late the same afternoon, John Payne turned left, away from the main road. The condition of the tar-macadam quickly deteriorated.

'Where are we going?' said Laura.

'Milton.'

'But, isn't it that way?'

'It can be.' He winked, smiled his victory smile. 'I discovered this last time I was up, can't believe nobody told me about it. Don't know why the builders didn't use it either, makes no sense at all.'

A hundred yards ahead was a dark green wall into which the track they were on disappeared. It looked to Laura as though they were heading into a Hansel and Gretel forest. Molly giggled as they bounced over the rough dirt surface. Laura was thinking that the pickup would finally justify itself when she saw the single storey, stone and wood building, set back off the road.

'Oh look, John, a cottage.'

'I think bothy is the word you're looking for. Or ruin.'

He had barely finished dismissing the building as abandoned when, over the dry stone wall, a twist of white smoke unwound in the breeze. Laura raised herself off the armrests to see over the wall. Standing in a clearing, amongst rows of beehives, a man in protective headgear lifted the lid off one of the hives. Maybe he looked at them before disappearing. He certainly paused, shrouded in a pale cloud, before he bent to look into the hive. She couldn't be sure.

'Look Molly, look.' Laura leant over the back seat, pointing out of the window, 'bee man – see – bee man.'

He was already invisible by the time Molly strained her neck so that she could see around the headrest of her child seat. 'Beeman.'

'Yes, bee man,' laughed Laura at Molly's response. She ran her finger up and down Molly's leg, 'Bzzzzzz, bzzzz, bzzzz,' causing another fit of giggles that should have been infectious.

'Shit. I thought that old place was empty.'

'Obviously not; and mind your language.'

'You can see it from the sunroom.'

'Really,' said Laura, looking back over her shoulder, 'I think it's sweet. It's got character.'

'I think you mean it needs attention.'

'It's just a bit ramshackle, that's all. Do you think he lives on his own?'

'Who knows?'

John sounded deflated. He was staring into the rearview.

'Pee'd off?'

'Not really, just thought we had the place to ourselves. Felt private, you know what I mean?'

'I think 'exclusive' is what you mean.'

'Is that wrong?'

'Come on, he might be nice.'

'You're right,' said John. 'We'll find out later, pay him a

visit. What do you think? Introduce ourselves to our surprise neighbour?'

'Good idea. Mmm, just think though, fresh honey for breakfast, still in the comb, lovely.'

'Beeman,' said Molly, delighted with her new word, 'bzzzzz, bzzzz, bzzzzz'

As Laura turned around to play with Molly, the track plunged into the trees. It was dark in an instant. Molly stopped talking. Her mouth hung open as she stared out of the window at the black branches reaching like arms through occasional flashes of sky, their spindly hands ready to snatch. She started as they brushed and screeched against the truck's windows. When she looked at Laura, her bottom lip was on standby and her eyes were swimming.

'Hey, it's okay,' she said. Laura gave Molly's leg a reassuring squeeze even though her own skin prickled. The conifers were well-established and had been planted close together. Barely any light made it down to ground level. She shuddered as all about them, the shadows twisted into shapes, swollen tongues in drooling mouths. Twigs cracked under-tyre as a creature heavy and thirsty roared through the trees; shaking the earth. Beyond their field of vision, a blacker black travelled deep in the undergrowth, its sharp eyes set above grinding white teeth, keeping easy pace with them, timing the pounce, gaining, looking to pick off the weakest, the juiciest, the most deserving. 'It's just trees, darling, we're in the forest.' She pulled a wide-eyed face for Molly, 'Spooky.'

'Pooky,' said Molly, unconvinced, her attention returning to the outside even as she drew her head backwards behind the headrest of her safety seat.

'You could have warned us,' said Laura, 'Jesus, I wouldn't come in here on my own. How long does it go on for?'

'It takes us all the way to Milton, about a mile. It runs between the two mountains, along the line of cleavage if you like, comes out at the back of the town, where that little church is. Remember – mid way up the hill?'

'No, not really.'

'I think it's brilliant. It cuts out that whole corner of the main road.' John turned the headlights on. 'That better?'

It wasn't. The beams picked out the matt bark of the trunks that lined the track and defined their way; made lurid the odd clump of mossy green that survived in the gutter, where winter's water had stagnated into an oily witch's brew. In the sub-canopy gloom however, their light was all but devoured. What had been black and hidden was shown to be a dry, dusty lair, alien and absorbing. Laura closed her eyes. If she didn't look, nothing could stir.

'Pooky.'

She wondered what was forming in her child's mind. Would this journey, her first from her new home, follow her for the rest of her life, ever ready to touch her on the shoulder?

'You want the inside light on?'

'No,' said Laura. She didn't say why. 'No.'

'You okay?'

'I'm fine,' she replied.

'You don't look it.'

'It's the dark, you know that.'

'Yes, but I didn't think…'

'It's not your fault.' She put her hand out and he took it, wrapping his fist around her fingers. They continued like this until she felt the pressure on her hand increase as he tightened his grip.

'It's okay to look,' he said.

Opening her eyes, she was facing up through the sunroof, beyond the ever-brown and evergreen to the flicker of heavenly blue that sped by, high above. When she lowered her head it was like looking through an ancient mystical doorway; a woodcut, a rough gothic arch of trunk and bough, guiding them out of the dread. Within a swirling veil of mist, like the focus of a fine summer snow globe, sat the little church, like a guardhouse at a border crossing, framed slightly to the left, as though making way for their exit. John put the windows down as they passed through the spray. It was cool on her face. The wipers automatically swept the coalescing droplets from the windscreen. She flinched at the sudden loud rush of the waterfall that fell on John's side and disappeared beneath them, reappearing way below to Laura's side as a broad stream. They had passed the carved wooden signpost before she had a chance to read it. Ahead, the opening was a clear sky that rushed over them as they were delivered back into the day.

Pulling the truck over, John stopped a few yards past the church, crushing the daffodils on the verge. He grinned at Laura, victorious.

'Worth it?' He pulled the handbrake and selected neutral.

She leant forward in her seat until her belt reached its limit. The sun through the screen warmed her and the goose-bumps subsided. She let the belt take her weight. She exhaled without knowing she had been holding her breath.

'Maybe.'

The glacial valley ran from left to right. Its broad, flat

bottom was a verdant canvas of farmland, marshland and common pasture, slashed with rusting fences, corrugated outbuildings, reed beds, ox-bow lakes and the erratic thread of the river. In the foreground, hemmed in by the rail-track that hugged the valley edge, the slate roofs of Milton shone in the summer day. Vehicles using the main road through the valley, the route of which mimicked that of the railway, disappeared into the village for a while before most of them emerged from the other side. Those that didn't dispersed into the dozen or so streets, lanes and dead ends that radiated from the main road like fish bones.

'Impressed?'

'It's magical,' said Laura.

'Isn't it just?' He rested his arms across the steering wheel. 'Recognise anything?'

Laura tried to identify some of the buildings. This was only the third time she had seen Milton, the first time from this vantage.

'Well, that's the 1970s school.'

'Ugly and out of place but with a good reputation,' they both chimed, smiling at each other.

'And, they must be the two hotels, the big roofs at that junction. The tourist office is opposite one of them, next to that café, Gilly's. There's the playground and the shinty pitch. And that's the church, obviously. The club house of the golf club, where the flagpole is...'

'Two hundred pounds a year and no joining fee.'

'Really? We should...'

'We already have.'

'Well done.' Laura stretched to see further to her right. 'Around that corner, the truck stop, the garage and the fire station, you can just see the practice tower. And they, 'she said, pointing across the valley, to the three tallest peaks that rose before them, 'are Creag Mhor, Creagh Dhubh and Creag Bheag, tallest to smallest.'

'Well done you. Not bad, for a third visit.'

'Google Earth.'

'That's cheating.'

'I was excited. Still am.'

'Me too.'

She kissed him.

They spent the next hour raiding the shelves of the main shop, a general store with a deli counter and a well-stocked wine aisle. They were impressed at the quality and range of goods they carried, almost as good as their city local. Laura lost count of the times she said, 'Oh look, they've got this,' and how often John said, 'this place must be a goldmine.' They spent a lot. He picked two assorted cases of wine, one white, one red, and a bottle of Pol Roger. She filled a trolley to overflowing with basics and essentials. He parked on double yellows outside the store and helped the staff load everything into the truck while she changed Molly's nappy in the staff toilet. They waved as they drove away.

'What lovely people,' said Laura.

'Yeah, seem so. Though if I'm spending that much in their shop I'd expect lovely to be the very least they could manage.'

'John. Honestly, I don't think that would matter. It was nice of them to let us use their rest-room.'

'I guess.'

'You know, I was so relieved when she was only wet.'

'Yup, that would have been bad form,' said John, chuckling, turning off the main road, climbing out of Milton, 'stinky nappy on the first visit.'

'And what were you like? You don't think you missed anybody out, do you?'

'Sorry?'

'Is there anybody you didn't tell?'

'Tell what?'

'Who we were – where we lived.'

'What do you mean?'

'Well, it just seemed, as though you wanted everybody to know, straight away. They'll find out soon enough. No need to be…'

'What?'

'So obvious,' she said.

'Obvious?' He glanced at her. 'You're right. I should have made them all guess who we are, where we live, how old Molly was.' Laura was smirking but refused to look at him, even as he leant closer. 'Do you think that would make me more endearing, less embarrassing?'

'Shut up. You know what I mean.'

'I do,' he said, 'but it's me. Never been one for mystique, you know that. Anyway, it's done. They know who we are.'

'Oh, they know.'

Laura said nothing else. Up ahead she could see the little church that had appeared to welcome them back into the light. What had filled the exit from the track was now dwarfed by the mountainside, a pinpoint of hope dominated by the mass above it. The smallest of landslides could take it away. Her chest tightened.

'You want me to turn around,' he said, 'go the long way?'

She looked in her mirror. Molly was sleeping.

'No, I'll get used to it.'

'You don't have to.'

'I want to. Keep going.'

John drove slowly in consideration of their daughter's rest. As they passed back through the spray of the falls, Laura noticed the sign pointed up the hill, against the flow. It said 'Piper's Pool'. She thought that sounded sweet and made a mental note to find it as she tried to relax and concentrate on the quiet, but the shadows deepened when her eyes were closed.

He paused, holding the knife mid-stroke. For the second time that day Luther felt the vibrations of a passing vehicle. He waited, hands steady, knowing it was them. When the tremors had settled he continued, sliding the edge across the whetstone, away from himself, honing off the burr. Satisfied when the edge popped the hairs from his arm, he placed it in the sheath hanging on the cellar wall next to an axe, a scythe and a machete. Below the blades, along the bench, a handful of rabbit skins lay on their boards, curing.

Upstairs, he brewed coffee and drank it as he watched them unload their truck, carrying even more boxes and bags into the house. Maybe the space intimidated them. They already had more than they needed. The child wandered around the house, exploring. The man brought her back to the sunroom, pointing at her and then the floor as he admonished her for straying. This happened three times. Then he placed her in a play pen too small to play in until they were ready to play with her. Luther's second cup had cooled before she rescued the child as he poured champagne. They touched glasses, kissed and drank. They sat on the sofa and talked. The man pointed in the direction of Luther's home. The woman stood up and walked to the glass wall. Her hair was long, kinked at the bottom, the way he had always liked. It swung as she turned to the man and said something. He finished his drink in one gulp, went into the old Macpherson house and reappeared with a bottle of wine, which he handed to her.

Three minutes later they knocked on Luther's door.

'Hello,' said the man, pushing his hand out. 'My name's John Payne. This is my wife Laura. We're your new neighbours.'

Luther shook the offered hand, providing ample resistance to the man's over-strong grip. He knew it was the last time they would shake hands.

'The holiday home?' said Luther.

'Oh, no, our home; we're here for good. This is where we live. Except when I have to go back to the city, for meetings, boring stuff like that. I expect I'll be away a few days a week.'

Luther nodded.

'Sounds like a holiday to me.'

'Do you mind if I ask your name?' said the woman, trying to be pleasant. 'Our daughter calls you the beeman.'

'Beeman's fine,' he said, bending down to the girl. 'Hello there.' She was unsure. One of her curls wound into her eye, causing her to blink. His natural instinct was to brush it aside. He pushed his hands into his pockets and pulled their lining tight into his fists. 'Aren't you beautiful?'

'Bzzz – bzzz,' said Molly.

'Yes, bzzz – bzzz,' copied Luther. The little girl smiled at him and he smiled back. 'And who are you?'

'This is Molly,' said the man, way above Luther's head.

'I was talking to Molly. Wasn't I, Molly?'

'She's been told not to talk to strangers.' The man placed a hand on Molly's head, as though to protect her from him.

'You know how it is?'

Luther stood up, leaving his smile with Molly.

'I thought we were neighbours.'

'Ah,' said the man, taking his hand off Molly and pointing at Luther, his fingers imitating a pistol being fired, 'got me.' He was half grinning, as though this were a game.

Luther noticed the woman shift awkwardly and glance up at the man, annoyed at his clumsiness. He could tell by the way that she held out the bottle of wine that it now felt to her like an apology she had to make on the man's behalf. He wondered how much space she had that was hers.

'We thought you might like this, a getting to know you present.'

'I might,' said Luther, accepting the bottle, reading the label. He looked at the woman. 'Thank you.'

'You're welcome.' A couple of seconds passed. 'Something smells nice,' she said, glancing into his home.

'Rabbit.'

'Really? Not something I've ever had, rabbit. Food of the future, they say?'

'Really?' said Luther.

She met his gaze.

'Anyway,' said the man, picking Molly up, making ready to leave, 'we just...' He stopped mid-sentence as Luther left them alone, going inside without a word of explanation. Before they could decide if they should stay or go, he returned with two skinned rabbits and held them out to the woman.

'Luther. Now we know each other.'

She didn't hesitate in taking the rabbits. Luther thought she would.

Laura put the scraped Creuset casserole into the dishwasher, the rabbit bones into the bin and The Silver Spoon onto the kitchen bookshelf. She wiped the base and the Aga brand new clean. Splitting the remains of the wine between their two glasses she took them into the sunroom. She heard the already familiar creak of one of the spiral stairs as she put them on the glass coffee table between the two sofas. John came around the corner and signalled that Molly was asleep.

'Fast?'

'Snoring like a motorbike,' he said. 'You should hear her.'

'I'm not surprised,' she said, stretching, arching over the sofa back exposing a strip of her tummy, 'it's been a long day for her.'

'Long day for us all.'

John slumped into the second sofa, lifted his wine and held it out for Laura to lift hers and ching against his, a delicate crystal ring.

'Cheers,' she said, 'happy new home.'

'Happy new wife.'

'You mean life?' she said, quicker than she would have wished.

'That's what I said, wasn't it?'

'You said wife.'

'I did?'

Was he smiling? Was that a slip? She kept her eye on him, looking for clues.

'Fatigue, I'm tired. Seriously though – well done us.' He took a glug of wine and relaxed, resting his head into one of the deep feather cushions.

She couldn't be sure if he was playing with her, laying down some new law. They sat in silence for a while, sipping wine, facing out. The day had darkened. The last of the sun caught the ripples across the lochan surface and the striped vertical face of the rushes along its eastern shore before leaving them to their first night.

'How old do you think he is?' said Laura.

'Who?'

'Luther.'

'I don't know, fifty, fifty-five?'

'No.' she said, 'not even fifty, if that.'

'If you say so.' John continued to look straight ahead. 'Does it matter?'

'No,' she said. 'I just wondered.'

The onset of the dark was the signal for the confused fluttering and crawling of winged nightlife to gather on the glass, attracted to the interior lights.

'Jesus,' said John, 'look at that. We're being invaded.'

They went to the wall and stood fascinated, as though attending some organised entomological performance: the dusty under-wing sheen of moths, the iridescent glint of compound eyes and blue black thorax, the pin-pricks of light from translucent wings.

'Do you know one thing we didn't think of?' said John, answering before she had time to think let alone answer, 'Screen doors; to keep the beasties out, midges mostly I'd say.' He went to slide a door open.

'No. You'll let everything in.'

'True,' he said, eyeing the floor outside. 'We could still fit them, a separate unit, like secondary glazing. Should do the trick don't you think?'

'Maybe, if you think it's worth it.'

'Well, no point having windows you can't open, is there?'

'Wouldn't they block the view?'

'Nah. I'll get them fitted so they don't. You just need to be clear about your specifications.'

They were getting screen doors.

Luther climbed out of the dream, lifting his head from the pillow as though to disengage, pushing the covers away. Absent for a long time, she had found him tonight, had been about his head like a caul, stifling him with smells and tastes long past. Her touch had crept all over him, raising the hairs on his body, rippling shivers across his shoulders. He put his feet on the cool of the floor and sat until he was alone again and the desire was gone.

His bladder was full. In the bathroom blood ribboned through his water and pinked the yellow in the bowl before it was flushed away.

It was early, the birds still silent, when Luther started his walk up the steep rise behind his home. He walked without light, treading a known path. Before long, he came to where the mountainside lost its shape and the knee of stone jutted out from its dark apron, a pale, grey marker. Passing behind it he turned into the trees, brushing through the soft fronds of new growth at the branch ends, fresh luminous fingers of needles reaching out from a murky, other place. Two black bands on a frosted bough betrayed the pre-dawn perching of a bird, its feet still warm from the roost. He followed the beam of his head-torch, working his way towards the distant tumble of the stream, making its way down to Milton where the waterwheel stole its life for the benefit of undemanding tourists and those who provided shoddy welcome for the price of a bed and breakfast.

Standing on the bluff that overhung the cascade, Luther watched the stream drop over sixty feet in a hundred yards. Curtains of water spilled over ancient strata until a cleft in the rock channelled each separate splash into one flow that plunged into the frothing pool that then spilled over the shallow basin. Above him, through the gap in the trees the sky had coloured with the dawn. He pushed his head-torch into his satchel.

Downstream, standing on a flat ledge of rock, he assembled his rod and organised his line. With the fly just resting on the water he readied himself. Raising the rod, using the tension from the surface, he formed a semi-elliptical D-loop with the line, which lifted the fly, taking it backwards, to be cast high and forward across the pool. The fly momentarily kissed the water where it eddied above a deep rock bucket, before being whipped from the surface as the rod was re-raised and re-cast, each kiss a chance.

Morning was established before the guts and gills of four brown trout spilled into the current, circling downstream as Luther rinsed their body cavities clean.

Filleted, pin-boned and grilled. Luther ate his breakfast standing as he watched John washing his truck as puffs of dust rolled through the heat-haze. He had his back turned to Laura. Neither saw Molly, wandering in the tall grass. Laura came through the door of the old Macpherson place barefoot in T-shirt and shorts, a skip in her step. She flattened the empty box she carried and added it to the pile by the porch door. Her hands behind her head, pulling her short ponytail in two so as to tighten the elastic bobble at its root, she looked bra-less. She glanced around, called. After a few seconds she called again. Unanswered, she pulled the door open and she leant out. The man looked at her over his truck. Luther opened his window. The curtain wafted as though pushed by the words as he heard her ask the man if Molly was with him.

'I thought she was with you.' The man stood up, wringing the final drops from his chamois as they spoke.

'I told her to stay in the sunroom.'

'When will that girl learn to do as she's told?'

'John, she's not even two.'

'She needs to learn.' He threw the leather into the bucket of water. 'You checked upstairs?'

'The gate's on,' said the woman turning back inside, skipping down the length of the sunroom and out of view, calling the child's name. The man walked the house's exterior walkway in the opposite direction. Luther wondered if they would acknowledge each other when they met on the other side.

Luther, distracted by the woman, hadn't noticed Molly's progress. She was across the bridge and halfway along the boardwalk over the lochan when Luther dropped his part-washed plate back into the sink. He was out of his door and through his gate before the man completed his circumference of the house to see Molly leaning out over the water, hunkered down, intent upon her own reflection; the water boatmen amongst the lily pads or some silvery flash of fish belly that had caught her eye yet now eluded her. Luther stopped, his legs in spasm in a childlike dance of fear as he willed the man not to shout.

'Molly' split the air like a gunshot and she was felled,

falling onto her nappy before tipping sideways, her head
smacking the planking as the man leapt onto the bridge. She
was already crying when the man struck her hard across the
legs, bellowing warning and instruction at her, his face inches
from hers as though he were inducting a raw recruit into army
life. Even he recognised the change of pitch in the child's
screaming, from shock to hysteria, as her understanding
of the situation vanished. He pulled her close as though
to smother the howling. The baby didn't want his comfort
and wouldn't be calmed. She kicked and pushed away from
him, terrified arms reaching for the woman running towards
them. Luther didn't know how much the woman had seen.
From her reaction he guessed she had witnessed everything.
She hit the man.

'What the fuck do you think you're doing – she's a baby
for Christ's sake.'

The man didn't resist as she took Molly from him. 'Don't
you ever lay a fucking hand on her again – look at the size of
you – you could kill her.'

He bristled at his daughter's eagerness to go to her and
his expression showed that he resented the small arms now
clamped around the woman's neck.

'I might have just saved her life, she was leaning over.'

'You hit her.'

'She needs to learn, she needs to be scared of the water.'

'She's scared of you. Look at her. What did you think you
were doing?'

The woman turned her back on him and left, squeezing
reassurance into a child already firmly attached.

'I was scared,' said the man.

She continued without turning back.

The man arched his back and ran his hands through his hair and dug his nails into his scalp, his face up to the sun, eyes closed.

When he brought his head back down he did a double take at something in the corner of his eye. He was staring directly at Luther. Luther stared the man down, only moving when the man looked away and headed home.

Molly sat on the kitchen counter next to the sink getting close to the final sob as Laura held a cold flannel over the vivid handprints on Molly's thigh. Thick red bars of impact and pain the width of his fingers.

'That better?'

Molly nodded, all the while looking at her thigh, fascinated by the marks. She mumbled something that Laura didn't catch.

'What? Molly, what did you say?'

'Sorry.'

'No,' Laura bent to Molly's level and held her shoulders. 'No. Molly's a good girl. Daddy is sorry.'

She didn't understand.

'Daddy naughty?'

'Today, yes.'

Laura stood up at the sound of his footsteps in the sunroom.

'Not now, John.'

'Laura.'

'I need time. We need time.'

He stopped. His breathing was still irregular.

'I was scared.'

He was just around the corner yet he didn't sound close at all.

'I know,' she said, her tone responding to the regret in his voice. 'Listen, we need milk.'

'I'll go.'

'That would be good.'

'Okay. Back soon.'

'Okay.'

John's boot-soles squeaked on the wooden flooring as he retreated to buy milk that both of them knew they didn't need.

The roar of the truck as it sped past, with its attendant spitting of gravel caused Luther to tighten. Although glad to be distracted from the depleted interior of the hive, he resented how strong and instant his reaction to the man was. It suggested the man was in control. He lowered the roof of the hive, left his smoker on the floor and lifted his veil away from his face as he walked to the house.

The teeth of the chainsaw glinted diamond sharp in the sun as Luther approached the pyramid of seasoned tree trunks by the rear gate. They turned into a quicksilver necklace as the chain was brought to speed and applied to the restraining posts. Woodchip sprayed like sparks as the saw ate through. Using one of the posts as a lever, Luther teased the pile from behind until it tumbled from the verge with the clunking rumble of some great glockenspiel. By the time John drove out of the trees on his way back from Milton, timber lay all over the lane. The truck came to a halt and he got out, talking loudly into his mobile phone. Luther carried on as though John wasn't there, slicing through one of the trunks he had supported in the two x-frames of a saw-horse, reducing the tree to fire-sized logs.

'No not at all, that's great news, I didn't expect you home for months, what happened – it's always complicated, does she have a name? – Okay, tell me about it when you get here – of course, no, I'll get you at the airport – absolutely, yes. Listen I'll call you in the morning, I need to get rid of some logs, – no, no, it can't wait, they're all over the lane. Right, speak in the morning, bye.'

John put his phone in his pocket and walked to the tree trunks that had blocked his way. Luther lifted his visor and pulled his ear-guards down around his neck. He approached, chainsaw idling in his hands. John looked up at Luther, still smiling from his phone call.

'Getting ready for the winter already, huh?'

Luther watched as John hauled one of the trunks to the side of the road.

'What are you doing?' he said.

'Well I would have thought that was obvious, I'm lifting the logs out of the way.'

'There's no need.'

'What?'

'It's my wood, it's on my road. I'm happy that it stays there.'

John straightened and looked at Luther as though he was expecting him to break into a smile, a sideways grin of nascent friendship. When Luther didn't smile, John looked bemused.

'I'm happy to give you a hand; come on,' he said, 'it'll be quicker with the two of us.'

'I'm in no hurry.'

'But I won't be able to get past if we don't move them.'

John bent to the task, straining as he pulled another of the trunks into the roadside, alongside a shallow drainage ditch.

'You should go around,' said Luther.

'What? The other way? That's seven miles.'

'Yes, it is.'

'Come on, that's time, not to mention the fuel; you need to think about the environment.'

Luther's stare moved to the vehicle, engine still running, then back to John who straightened himself again, realizing that Luther was being serious.

'Come on – we're neighbours, let's get along.'

Luther considered this for an instant and knew that even if he had wanted to, it was unlikely he could ever be neighbourly with this man. He'd done talking about the timber.

'Don't hit your daughter.'

'What?'

'Neighbourly advice.'

John's face clouded over as he approached.

'Is that what this is about?'

Luther drew the chainsaw between them, the steady kick of its motor now loaded with menace, filling the air between them. John stopped. His eyes darkened to those of an enemy. He clenched his fists, knuckle-white and impotent, swayed with anger.

'I don't want or need your fucking advice. I know how to treat my family.'

'Really?'

John strode back to his truck and climbed in, slamming the door. The passenger window slid down and he glared at Luther. 'Why are you being like this?' When Luther didn't respond he shook his head, revved the engine hard and drove at the logs. The wheels spun against the first tree trunk causing it to bounce up against the underside of his front bumper. Just as Luther thought that John was going to be made to look foolish there was a change in the register of the engine as he engaged four-wheel drive and the tyres gripped, pushing and pulling the truck over, giving it momentum enough to bounce over the others and speed the hundred yards to his driveway, narrowly missing the gate post as he swerved the vehicle through, onto the safety of his own property.

Crunching to a halt, John threw his door open and jumped out to inspect the front of his truck. The swearing, kicking of the ground and the slamming of the truck door brought the trace of a smile to Luther's face. He turned the chainsaw off as John stormed into the house. He could hear the cry of coot chicks, grasshoppers about his feet, the buzz of a scouting bee, the blood in his veins.

Laura poured John a beer.

She waited as he sat at the breakfast counter doing the breathing through his nose routine that he always did when he wanted people to know he was angry, as though he was containing himself for their benefit. As if that was a possibility. He had apologised to Molly, now it was his turn.

'Here, drink this, calm down.'

'I am calm.'

'I just think you should give it a day at least before you go charging back over there,' she said.

'And take a weapon?'

'I'm sure he didn't mean it that way.'

'You didn't see him.'

'Maybe speak to somebody in the village before you do anything, find out a little more about the man, his situation. What about Mr Cargill?'

'Mm.'

She pushed the phone across to him.

'Oh, by the way,' he said, 'Frank's coming up tomorrow.'

'Oh shit John, we've hardly moved in ourselves.'

'I know, I know. It'll be fine. He's only here for a few days. He has to go back out next week.'

'I thought he was out there for six months.'

'Supposed to be. Seems he's been transferred to another field and he's got a few days between jobs. Come on, what did you want me to say to him? 'No Frank, it's not a good time for us at the moment." He looked at her as though it was unreasonable for her to expect him to have the answers.

'Well, it isn't. Why has he been moved?'

'I don't know, he'll tell us tomorrow. You know what he's like.'

'Exactly,' she said. 'Exactly.'

'I know.' He picked up the handset. 'Come on, let's get this over with.'

Laura felt like crying as she watched John punch in the solicitor's number.

When Cargill answered she pressed the speaker button, wanting to be part of the call rather than be alone with her thoughts.

'Cargill, this is J.P.'

'J.P. How are you enjoying the new home?'

'Why didn't you tell us about our neighbour?'

She had been right about Cargill; he had plenty to say

about Luther. John was stunned when Cargill informed them that not only did Luther own the stretch of road outside his house, he owned it for the length of his property, which included the track that ran through the twenty acres or so of woodland that stretched almost all the way to the village. It was a private road.

'But what about right of way; he's not above the law, surely?'

'He ignores it,' said Cargill. 'I don't even think he'd allow the hearse through anymore, assuming it could make the journey. You've seen the way he's allowed the track to grow over and run to ruin.'

'I'll speak to him,' said Laura.

'I wish you luck, Mrs Payne.'

'How do you mean?'

'Do you really think you're the first people here who would rather drive one mile than seven?'

'Others have had the same problem?'

'Luther likes his privacy.'

'I don't want to intrude,' said John, 'I just want to get into Milton.'

'I suggest the road, it's safer.'

John mimed the word 'safer' to Laura, his hands open, palms up, in a 'what the fuck does that mean' gesture. She shook her head, her hands mimicking his.

'J.P., you still there?'

'Yes,' said John. 'When did he buy it?'

'Fifteen, sixteen years ago.'

'Mr Cargill,' said Laura, 'why didn't you tell us this?'

'Slipped my mind.'

John looked at the speakerphone, disbelieving.

'You cunt.'

'John.'

'He set us up. Cargill, you are a cunt.'

It took Cargill a moment to reply. They heard a muffled sigh as though he was drawing his hand over his mouth before admitting the truth.

'Maybe, but I'm a little bit richer than I was and I've offloaded the property that had been on my books the longest. A property I had resigned myself to never selling. Caveat emptor, J.P. If you'd asked me I'd have told you, but you didn't. Besides, you can afford the fuel, and the time. Your phone is your office, as you have reminded me so often over the last year.'

John punched the phone off.

'Fuck. These fucking people.'

She sat thinking about Frank's visit as she watched John stride up and down not knowing what to do with his anger, looking for some release. When he picked Molly up from where she had been playing away with boxes in the corner Laura knew he didn't want to be angry. He changed visibly, his shoulders rounding and his neck becoming flexible again as he buried his head in his daughter, who held him. She had forgotten the smack. When he finally achieved stillness he was standing in front of the glass wall, focused on the entrance into the woods, his anger channelled into a decision.

'The hell with it,' he said, 'we'll just buy the track off him, the land as well if we need to. We can afford to do that, even if it's only to win.'

'Really?'

'Yeah.'

'We'll give him full access rights, on paper, so there are

no hard feelings, no misunderstandings. You never know, it might even do us some good with the fine people of Milton, they can't all be cunts like Cargill.'

'John, will you stop using that word.'

'It's okay, she doesn't understand.'

'She can hear. And anyway, I do and I don't like it.'

'Okay. You're right, I'm sorry. Just wound up, that's all.'

'I know. What if he won't sell?'

He laughed. 'You've seen the hovel he lives in. He needs our money. He'll snatch our hands off, you watch.'

'And if he doesn't?'

'He'll have a price; we all do.'

Laura didn't think he would. She had no right to this conviction, having only met him once, but she felt that the man with the bees, skinned rabbits, strong arms and sharp, sad eyes would win.

She was up all night with Molly. The child was unsettled, wouldn't take a bottle, wouldn't stay in her cot and cried every time she was left alone. John suggested teething before he went back to sleep and heavy snoring. Laura believed it was the day; their arrival, the forest journey, the fear, pain and confusion of that moment at the lochan floating back to the surface of her tired mind, looking for answers. Empathy bound them. The writhing dark of Laura's memories had kept her from sleep untold times. Though Molly's arrival had reduced their frequency, she still woke when that night recurred; the backwards jerk of her neck, struggling to breathe through the leather glove clamped across her mouth and nose, losing her balance as she was dragged from the pavement, the knife to her throat, the blade breaking her skin as she was tripped and pushed down between the wheelie bins, her face forced into the used smell of the alley floor, cigarette stubs between the cobbles, flattened bottle tops and crushed glass; diesel flowers floating on rain-diluted piss. Keening as she was entered from behind, the security lights above the rear doors of the bars reflected in the blade of the knife.

She took Molly downstairs. They spent the night together in the snug, pyjamaed, organizing the bookshelves into alphabetical order, looking at the pictures stacked against each other waiting to be hung, listening to music, drinking milk as they watched the morning news, all as though they were equals, inpatients at some private clinic of bad dreams.

Laura grilled John a cooked breakfast. Molly was yawning and gurning on the floor, tearful and bad tempered, pushing away toys and squishing pieces of fruit between her fingers. Laura was holding off on another morning bottle until she was in her seat, nappy changed and ready to go. It was a couple of hours to the airport and back, so she would go with her dad to pick up Frank. She needed to sleep.

The bottle she had practically snatched from Laura was almost finished by the time John had her strapped in and had kissed Laura.

'Drive carefully.'

'Don't I always? You get to your bed, you look exhausted.'

'I wonder why.'

He kissed her again.

'See you soon.'

She kissed Molly and waved to them as he bumped out onto the main road and headed north.

The sap-sweet smell of fresh cut wood travelled on the

breeze. Logs had fallen into an ad hoc pile beneath the end of a complete trunk, waiting on the saw horse. Trees still blocked their access to Milton. It was obvious to her that Luther had stopped when he'd made his point. For all she knew they would lay there all year, uncut, unused.

She knocked on his door. No answer. She knocked again. Before long she heard the scrape of a chair, footsteps that stopped behind the door. It was a few seconds before the door opened. Why was she nervous? He had been nice to her. He looked surprised and she guessed he was expecting John, with an apology maybe, or further argument.

'Hello Luther.'

'Hello,' he replied, 'I thought it might be...' and his sentence tailed off as he looked down the path to the new house.

'Just me I'm afraid. John's gone to the airport. He took Molly with him. I thought I could come and apologise for his behaviour, whatever it was he said.'

Once he had established that she was alone his face softened, and Luther looked pleased to see her there, if a little uncomfortable. He appeared to be struggling with something as though he couldn't make his mind up, biting his bottom lip, glancing away from her, studying the porch floor. Taking a step back from the doorway he gestured for her to go in.

It was warm inside. The room, a combined living and dining area, was Spartan and clean. On the far side the bare planks of the floor were offset by a tapestry rug in front of an old tan leather sofa beneath the rear window. An ancient cast iron stove squatted in the fireplace between two alcoves, one full of books, the other a store of dry logs. Three of the four chairs around the beaten pine dining table were pushed in tight. The fourth, facing out of the front window, had a jacket over its back. On the table were needle and thread and a shirt, mid-repair. Next to the shirt an A4 notebook lay open, a pen clipped onto the pages.

'I'm sorry, you're busy. I could…' She stopped when Luther dismissed the shirt with a wave of his hand that looked to her a little too casual.

'It can wait. It's only a button. I'm having coffee. Can I make you one?'

'Erm, yes. That would be nice, thank you.'

She followed him into the small kitchen area as he prepared the stove top brewer and put it on the Rayburn. Pans hung from hooks driven into the mortar of the exposed stone wall. A simple plank shelf held some eggs, basic condiments and a few plates and bowls. The underside of the shelf had hooks from which hung spoons, whisk, sieves and coffee mugs. Pots of herbs grew on the window-sill above the sink; basil, coriander and parsley. A handful of leaves, linear and deep green with a pale central stalk, like a writing quill, lay on the draining board. She picked one up.

'Try it.'

'Sorry,' she said, putting it back, 'I was just curious.'

He handed her the leaf.

'Try it, go on.'

She pinched the end off and nibbled it. It was slightly fibrous, pungent and unmistakable.

'Garlic?'

'Wild garlic, allium ursinum, just coming to the end of its season.'

'Mmm. I'm looking forward to picking it next year already.'

Putting the leaf back on the pile, the sparkle of water caught her eye and she looked out through the window. She was taken aback to find that not only could she see the boardwalk over their lochan, the long grass between it and their garden, but also the length of her summer room.

'My god, you can see right in.'

'If I look,' he said, handing her a coffee in a thick white mug. 'I like mine strong, tell me if you want some water in it.'

She took a sip and was surprised at how satisfying she found the bitterness.

'Good coffee, Luther, I'm impressed.'

'Thought you'd like it.'

Laura expected him to say something else as he paused, his cup just below his mouth. He didn't. He examined her. Her throat and neck prickled with rising warmth as she felt his eyes moving over her face and saw the developing pleasure he took in his inspection.

'Is something the matter?'

'No,' he said.

'You're smiling. What at?'

'You remind me of someone.'

'Really,' she said, trying to conceal her curiosity, 'in what way?'

'You're incandescent – in the same way she was.'

Hot coffee caught in the back of her throat and Laura coughed into her cup, splashing coffee up her face, onto the floor and down the front of her cardigan. She knew that she was blushing even as she wiped her face and hoped he would think it was the heat from the drink.

'Sorry, I wasn't expecting that. Give me a cloth, I'll wipe the floor.'

'Leave it.' He ran the cold tap and held his hand out as he rolled his sleeves up. 'Let me have your cardigan. Quickly, I'll soak it, stop it staining.'

Unbuttoning it as though she had no choice, Laura slipped it off and handed it to him inside out. Bubbles surfaced and burped as he plunged the lambswool into the sink of water, keeping it submerged as he massaged the stains away.

'Oh dear. That was embarrassing.'

'That wasn't my intention,' he said, lifting the cardigan, rolling it into a ball as it drained, exerting a constant pressure, forcing out the contained cascade, sounding like the rain sticks she had seen in charity shops. Watching how he kept his plastered thumb away, she traced the rivulets as they escaped through his fingers, over the back of his hands, trickling along the muscle contours of his arms to drip from his elbows. A heart tattoo with blurred names across it stuck out from beneath his shirt sleeve. It looked traditional on Luther, rather than hackneyed. The drops became singular; plip, plip, plip.

He relaxed. He held it out to her, shaking it from the shoulders, letting it fall back into shape.

'You can dry it over your Aga.'

About to take it from him, she paused, her look questioning him.

'I've seen it,' he said. 'Oil-fired, when you're surrounded by wood. That was a decision made in the city.'

'He thought it would be simpler, cleaner.'

'Clean? Take a look about you. Nothing's clean.'

She felt out of her depth, unsure if he was teasing her. He was right though, they had no idea about the realities of living more than walking distance from a bar, store or

43

restaurant. Where public transport, should they deem to use it, was regular and reliable and there was always a shop open, somewhere.

'I don't think that was fair.'

'What?'

'For you to be traipsing around my home,' she said, 'without me knowing, without being asked even.'

'It was only a house the last time I was in it, empty, and I was invited.'

'What, did John...?'

'Cargill. He treated it as though it was his. He is an envious man. He had the biggest house in the valley until you came along. But you're right,' he opened his arm across the room in a generous sweep of invitation. 'Look around.'

'Now you're being silly.'

'No. It's only fair. I sleep in there; I live in here; that's the bathroom.'

Laura didn't move. She took in the room. Beyond her initial impressions there was little else to add. It was self-contained and geared to function. Maintained rather than decorated. It felt empty to her, hollow even. Aside from the alcove of books there were no shelves, ornaments, pictures or mementos. There was no indication of any past at all. No place of storage.

'You don't have any cupboards.'

'True.'

'But, where do you keep things?'

'You mean stuff?'

'Yes, stuff you keep, like...'

'Nothing to keep. Besides, the less you have the less there is to keep tidy.'

'I can see the attraction in that,' she said. 'But, what about food? You can't go out and pick your dinner every day, surely?'

'Most days.' Luther finished his coffee. 'And when I can't,' he gestured with his cup to the stairs leading down to the cellar. The trap door was hooked open. It reminded her of the storm doors into the cellar in The Wizard of Oz, where Aunty Em and the family retreat to, leaving Dorothy to her fate in the approaching tornado. Her curiosity must have been obvious.

Luther draped the damp cardigan over the back of an unused dining chair, smoothing the shoulders flat before leading her down the steps.

It was the same size as the living room above. Dried herbs, chillies and strings of garlic and onions hung from nails. A workbench ran the length of both longer walls creating a galley effect. Boxes were piled against the end wall. Rabbit skins were spread on boards. Tools filled a rack and lanterns hung from pegs. Jars of what she initially took to be animal parts, until she recognised them as tomatoes in their own juice or vegetables in a clear liquid, vinegar or brine, were collected together away from the skins.

'Is there a draught?' she said, crossing her arms, covering her nipples, 'it's cold.'

'It's constant.'

He snapped open a safety strap and slid a knife from its sheath. She tensed as he walked towards her and the doubt must have been as obvious as her curiosity had been. Either that, or there was no hiding anything from this man. He put his hands up.

'What do you think I'm going to do?'

'I don't know. Nothing. Feels weird – being here.'

'Just relax, please. You're safe with me.'

Laura laughed and they both acknowledged the pantomime quality of his reassurance.

'Okay,' she said.

He untied a drawstring and lifted the muslin cover up over a smooth thigh of cured ham. He teased a petal of meat the colour of a rosehip from the leg and held it between fingertip and thumb, translucent beneath the glare of the bulb. Although Laura put her hand out to take it, he raised it to her mouth, his thumb brushing her bottom lip. She could feel the heat from his hand and hesitated momentarily before putting her tongue out in supplication. She sighed as it dissolved, the dense saltiness of the meat causing her mouth to salivate.

'My goodness.'

'I knew you'd like it.'

'It's amazing. You did it yourself?'

'Of course.'

He made her feel like an inductee. His direct stare was too much and she was back to feeling awkward. She moved over to the wall of the cellar, turning her back to him, her attention focused on what was stored in the rows of jars along the workbench. She read their labels out loud, commented on the quality and purity of the larder's preserves, jams and pickles as well as fruit and vegetables. She held a jar of blackcurrants up to the light to catch the midnight shine of their juice.

'They're gorgeous,' she said. 'Do you know that blackcurrants have a high antioxidant value? Good for your immune system, so they say.'

'It's more important they have a high flavour value, wouldn't you say? They need to taste good. Besides, you would have to eat a lot before they would be of any real benefit, and no amount could save you.'

Laura put the jar back down, thinking that this was a strange thing to say. Had there been a change in his voice? She couldn't be certain; it was slight if at all. She turned the jars so that all the date labels faced the front, doodled in the dust on the lids.

'You must be self-sufficient.'

'Almost.'

When she turned to face him he looked the same, sure of himself, blatant in his confidence, even dangerous, and she doubted she had heard the weakness in his voice.

'If I don't pick it, or kill it,' he said, opening the door to a tall metal locker, revealing three guns, 'I don't eat it. Except coffee, whisky. There's always something you can't do, or do without.'

She met his gaze again, dropped her hands to her sides, refusing to be intimidated. The hint of a smile spread across each of their faces.

'Do you mind if I ask you something?' she said.

'No.'

'Upstairs. Why are there are no photographs?'

It was almost imperceptible, but this time she had no doubt she had caught it, a change in his eyes like the momentary glide of a camera's shutter. A sliver of something had escaped.

'There are many,' he tapped against his temple, 'I see them every day.'

'Where is she now?'

'Gone.'

His voice was softer.

'You still have feelings?'

'Oh yes.'

Laura sensed that she, whoever she was, wasn't coming back.

'She's invisible; as though you're hiding her. If you weren't here, there would be no record of you either.'

'And no bad thing.'

There was a finality about this sentence that seemed to please him. He was smirking.

'What?' she said.

'You.'

'What about me?'

'A lot. An awful lot.'

His continued and unabashed inspection of her evidently gave him much to smile about, until he registered her scar.

'That looks fresh, a few months?'

Laura covered the glossy pink line on the side of her neck with her hair and broke eye contact.

'A year.' She paused. 'Just over a year.'

'You're a slow healer.'

'I don't really want to talk about it. I'm sorry, I should be getting back.'

Laura made for the stairs and Luther stood aside.

'Why did you come, really?'

'To talk about the road.'

'There's nothing to talk about,' he said, 'but I'm glad you came.'

She heard the clunk of the light-switch and the sound of his boots on the bottom steps as she left his house.

Luther looked at the cardigan drying over the back of the chair and saw her there. Her hair was dull and uncared for, a single elastic band holding it in a lank, greasy tail that hung over her shoulder. The nape of her neck was stiff, her back rigid, even as she lifted the glass to her mouth. He spoke to her but she refused to acknowledge him. He couldn't tell if she was still crying. He had known tears to roll down her raw cheeks for a whole day, onto her clothes, staining her breasts damp; a white salt frill drying around the outer edge as she sat into the night.

The first time she had poured whisky into her coffee she had joked that it was the only way to stop crying herself dry. He hadn't stopped her. She said it helped. It didn't help for very long and he had witnessed her falling apart with astonishing speed, rejecting his concern, comfort or consolation; closing all the doors and windows between them.

She had disappeared before him, a flower in autumn robbed of its petals, reduced to withered sepal, stamen and style; used, bearing no relation to the beauty that was. Her anguish had filled their house, leaving no room for his, which he had sealed and vacuumed, embarrassed by it in comparison to hers.

He sat at the table. Moving the chair to face his, he fastened the three mother of pearl buttons of the cardigan. Droplets still gathered and fell from the end of the arms. Lifting the needle caused the button to slide down the thread to its intended position on his shirt. He pushed the point of the needle through the blood-stained dressing on his thumb.

Molly stared at him the way she stared at a television screen or a load of washing turning in the machine, trying to work out what was going on, what made it work. She was mesmerised. Frank had been high-spirited since he had arrived, lifting Molly out of her seat and holding her high like a trophy as he walked into the house. John had trailed behind, man the hunter, a chill box of meat on his shoulder, Frank's bag in his hand.

John went through and dumped the meat in the kitchen. Frank put Molly down and replaced her with Laura, lifting her off the ground as he gave her a big hug and she gave him a peck on the cheek. The welcome over, Laura took his bag upstairs as John gave Frank a quick yet detailed tour of the downstairs. Frank nodded, looked at the views, agreed with John about the oak flooring and pronounced it a palace.

'Compared to the dump I've just spent the last two months in, anyway. Come on, show me upstairs later, let's hit the fridge; get the sand out of my pipes.'

Frank had half emptied his first bottle by the time John had the lid off his own. His exaggerated, 'AAAHHH,' made Molly smile. She sucked on the straw of her carton of juice and copied him, 'aaahhh'.

'So,' said John, 'you're home early because of the living conditions?'

'As if. You know me, I'll sleep anywhere.'

'And with anyone.'

'Well…'

'Go on.'

'One of my bosses, she objected to my extra-curricular activities, which was rich.'

'How so?'

'She was one of them, for a night anyway.'

'You slept with your boss?' said Laura, as she came into the kitchen.

'Amongst others. It got messy. She said I created an imbalance in the working environment.'

'You were only out there two months,' said John.

'Exactly. She rushed to judge me. I knew you'd understand.' He finished his second bottle. John drank most of his in one go just to keep up as Frank got two more from the fridge. 'What do they expect; middle of fucking nowhere, nothing to do but ping pong, the gym and women? It's always going to happen. An oilfield's the wrong environment for women, I've always said that. Guys just fight and get on with it. The work gets done.'

'I always said you should have been a soldier.'

'On the money they're paid? Besides, there are women soldiers.'

'Frank,' said Laura, 'you surprise me, so enlightened, practically a new man.'

'What can I say?'

'New man,' said Molly.

Frank looked at her.

'You talking to me?'

She wasn't sure enough to give a full smile.

'New man.'

Frank took a step towards her.

'You talking to me?'

Molly took a step away from Frank and looked up at Laura, taking courage from the fact that her mum was smiling.

'New man.'

'You,' said Frank, pointing at Molly as he stomped another step forward, 'talking to me?'

Molly squealed, turned and ran.

For the next few minutes, Frank chased Molly around the house and the garden like an uncle should. Laura knew when he jumped out and surprised Molly that he hadn't spotted the signs of fatigue or nervous fear, like a parent would. Molly vomited and started to cry. Frank lifted her by the oxters from behind and handed her to Laura with a 'what the fuck did I do?' look on his face as though it was Molly's fault; she wasn't tough enough.

'Whoops,' he said, 'didn't see that coming.'

'I did.'

With energy still to burn, Frank busied himself while Laura took Molly upstairs. As John mopped up the sick, checking to see if the floor had stained, Frank opened all the windows, refreshed their beers and refilled the fridge. He assembled the barbeque while John marinated the meat, only pausing to whistle in admiration at mother and child when they reappeared in fresh clothes. He finally relaxed, physically at least, six or seven beers into the afternoon, sitting on the grass with his back against a boulder, looking at the house.

'So how's business?' he said. 'How's the world treating J.P. Holdings?'

'It's good,' said John, 'really good. You haven't seen your account?'

'No, not for a while actually.'

Frank sat smirking in the silence. John turned the meat over.

'Your cut's been going in.'

'What John means,' said Laura, 'is that he's worked hard and is reaping the dividends. He's used your dad's money well. He's expanded the portfolio, initiated new funds and the return on your initial investment is already considerable.'

'With further potential,' said John.

'Listen to you, the richest man in Bedford Falls, wife, kid, fantastic house, surrounded by nature. And what have I got, apart from shitloads of money?' said Frank, chuckling.

John chuckled along with him as he returned the tongs to the meat.

'Shitloads of money and a perfect steak is what I'd say you have, listen.'

She'd lost count of how many times she'd told John not to do that, pressing down on the steak when it was cooking. He thought the sizzle was a good sign, an indicator of how juicy the meat was. He was right, but he was squeezing it all out. Each drop that hit the coals was a flame of lost flavour.

'John,' she said, 'you fancy getting me a top-up? I'll watch that.'

Frank jumped up, 'I'll get it.'

'No, I'll get it,' said John. 'You stay where you are, you're the guest.'

'The hell you will,' said Frank. 'You stay there, look after the meat. Women and barbecues don't mix, you know that.'

'True enough,' said John, giving Laura raised eyebrows in apology while Frank disappeared into the house. 'Frank's on it, Honey.'

'So I see. You think there was any chance he was being ironic?'

'Frank and irony? Women have more in common with barbeques.'

She was still giggling when Frank came back and popped the cork on another of the champagnes he'd brought with him. Molly watched as it travelled through the air, landing halfway to the lochan. She looked at Laura. Laura nodded; a wee wink, enough to bring a milk tooth smile to Molly's face as she got to her feet and went in search of the missing cork.

'John was telling me about your neighbour.'

'He means the arsehole.'

'John. That's not nice and it's not fair.'

'But it's true, from what John tells me.'

'You don't know that.'

'And you do?'

'I might.'

Laura regretted having said this even as Frank turned to John and hooked a thumb in her direction.

'Listen to her, little brother. Laura's been exploring.' His voice morphed into a nursery rhyme taunt. 'Laura's been exploring, Laura's been exploring.'

By which time John had forgotten the meat.

'You went to see him?'

'Yes, I went to see him.'

She was surprised how forcefully it came out and hoped it wasn't obvious to them that she would not be belittled by them. John didn't appear to notice.

'But, why would you do that?

'Well I just thought he might respond better to being talked to rather than shouted at.'

'But, I don't understand. Why would you go and see him without me? He could be dangerous.'

Laughing probably wasn't the best response, though Frank appreciated it. John, with one eye always on Frank, wielded the greasy tongs in her direction, drops of bloody meat juice catching the light as they fell into the grass at his feet.

'For fuck's sake, Laura, he came at me with a chainsaw.'

'Came at you? Come on, isn't that a bit…'

'Hey. You weren't there.'

She let it go, biting her lips tight-closed. She watched him as he sulked over the coals, pushing the steaks half an inch this way, half an inch that. She didn't share the image she had of John being chased by Luther.

'Did you go in?' said Frank. 'What's in his cellar, did you see in his cellar? John said the house is like the Evil Dead cabin.'

'Food,' she said, still eyeing John.

'What?'

'It's his larder.'

'You went into his cellar?' said John.

'Shit, no body parts, trapped teenagers, fridges full of heads?'

'Frank, will you grow up?' she said, before she shrieked, laughing again. Frank had bitten two eyes and a mouth from a tortilla and had it on as a mask. He did a note perfect impression of a Texas Chainsaw as he jumped up and swung his air weapon through Laura's midriff, Leatherface at large. Then, with his back to John, he stuck his tongue through the mask, pointed and flickering. Unaware, John saw Frank's fooling as his way back in and he shared in the joke, which for Laura had already run its length.

'So,' said John, 'what did he have to say for himself?'

'He's not interested in selling,' she said, prickling all over as she remembered the way Luther had made her feel, 'not interested at all.'

'You mention any figures?

'No.'

'He will be – money talks.'

Frank carried the Neil Diamond song like a batten, singing along as Laura's attention drifted towards the smoke coming over the wall of Luther's property, cotton-white against the gilded branches of the broom, diverging in the background like a pollen-heavy garden firework.

The unused flowers of the wild cherry fell like scented snow. Petals were dislodged, broken and dismembered by the breeze. They drifted against rows of earthed-up potatoes, glittered in the grass and flattened themselves against the hives in polka dot compensation for their inner night and to remind the bees they had been there. Lifting the roof, Luther was faced with the true nature of the hive. There had been no change since yesterday; they had gone. In past years, late May had seen combs full or filling with pollen and honey and the brood area expanded down throughout the empty combs in the lower chamber as bee numbers increased and their activity became delirious. This year there was nothing. He was steadily losing his entire stock. His colonies had disappeared or died, though where he didn't know; there was no sign of dead bees. He didn't believe they had swarmed; it was too early in the year. Survivors or stragglers wandered between the frames, distressed and aimless without a queen to service, cells to cap or young brood to tend to. The emptiness was contagious. Luther replaced the roof.

Only three of his forty hives contained colonies capable of producing honey come harvest time, if they were still here. He had cared for these creatures for almost thirty years, become immune to their stings and fed them through winters; found solace in the continuity of their swarm and dance lifecycle when his had been out of control. He resented their absence, feared the chaos that would come without routine and the responsibility of caring. Their mutual need had been their contract, surely. How could they abandon him?

Standing in the decimated apiary, surrounded by pointless blossom, Luther could discern the individual buzz of each surviving worker that flew by. To his eyes, their flight paths were uncertain, lacking purpose. The fearless confidence embodied in the hum of communal foraging that drilled through the summer like the drone of the bagpipe through a tune had left the garden. He sighed and took his veil off. Unzipping his boiler suit, he went inside to piss some blood.

Drinking whisky on the back porch, Luther heard their voices getting closer, discussing him, without her. He reclined into the evening shade of the porch as they came into view, keen to observe. They stopped at the logs in the road and the other one started to shake his head as though in disbelief.

'He really didn't want you to get past, did he?'

John snorted in response. The other one stood on one of the tree trunks and began rolling it with his feet, walking as a circus performer would, arms extended for greater balance. John tried three times to do the same but fell from his perch and gave up, affecting nonchalance. He stood with his hands deep in his pockets, his back to Luther, watching the other one show off.

'You've got no balance, never did. Remember the skateboard?'

'Yes,' said John, 'I remember the skateboard.'

'Broke it because you couldn't do it – wouldn't let anybody else have it.'

'It was mine.'

'I'd have liked it.'

'Too late.'

'I should've just taken it.'

'Too late.'

'Maybe,' said the other one as he began rolling the trunk underfoot, performing, pleased with himself. 'Anyway, who needs a skateboard?'

'There you go then,' said John, 'no harm done. It's in the past.'

'Talking of which, everything okay between you two, you know, since the thing, her affair?'

'It wasn't an affair, Frank. It was a one-off.'

'So she says.'

'And I believe her. So yes, everything is okay.'

'Fair play to you, John, I wouldn't have taken her back.'

'That's all over, finished. '

'You don't know that.'

'I do. We all make mistakes.'

'I guess. What comes around goes around though, that's something.'

John put his foot on the log, stopping its motion.

'Frank, what are you saying?' Frank turned to him. 'You think she deserved it?'

'That's not what I said, John. Although you have to admit it does have a karmic kind of balance to it.'

John kicked the log, almost toppling Frank.

'You are fucked, Frank. You know that?'

'Hey, I'm sorry. I didn't mean anything by it, it just...'

'Just what?'

'Seemed obvious. I'm sorry.'

'Obvious? Jesus, Frank. Is it any wonder you're single?'

'I said I'm sorry.'

He put his hands in his pockets and continued to roll, backwards and forwards in the silence between them.

'She's recovered though?'

'I would say so,' said John. 'She seems fine to me. She doesn't really talk about it.'

'You've asked her though, about it?'

'She knows I'm here. She'll talk when she's ready.'

'I suppose. You know her better than I do.'

Frank steadied himself and turned to John, squinting in the sun. Luther could see his face and the back of John's head.

'I'm sorry. I mean it.'

'I know,' said John.

'She's looking good now though, isn't she? Looks like country air agrees with her.'

Luther didn't like the way Frank grinned, or the length of time. It meant John was grinning back.

'Yeah, she is,' John said, 'she's looking good. I think moving here was definitely the right thing.'

Frank nodded, swatting a bee away. The angered bee came back, prompting more flapping, a loss of balance and a fall. He yelped as he hopped between the logs, one hand outstretched, this time for support instead of balance.

'Ah, fuck fuck fuck fuck, fucking logs.'

John gripped him, taking his weight as he tried to stand on his twisted ankle, swearing at the logs, the bee.

'You want to go back? I'll tell Laura to give us a lift, she won't mind.'

'No, no, let's carry on, it'll walk off.'

Frank planted his foot.

'The alcohol will kill the pain on the way back at least,' said John.

'Exactly, let's go see what Milton's got to offer as nightlife. Anyway, I want to see the 'pooky' woods you were talking about.'

'Wooooh.'

One hobbling, their arms around each other, they passed into the trees, giggling like schoolboys.

Luther smiled as he pushed the cork back into the whisky bottle.

Molly was already snoring. Laura leaned into the cot, pulled the cover over her shoulders and tucked her sheet under the mattress, replicating the swaddling that had been the key to getting her to sleep through the night as a newborn. Closing the blinds, she switched on the night-light on top of the chest of drawers, a single bulb inside a rotating fairground shade. Pale horses carouselled around her room, growing large and ill-defined the further they were from the lamp.

Laura sat on the single bed that Molly would soon move into and watched her sleeping. The cot was divided between baby and a small army of soft toys; between sleep and night-time watch. The alert glass eyes of teddy, lamb and jungle friends caught the light of the guardian horses as hers moved beneath untroubled lids, her lips still slightly parted in memory of feeding. Leaning in to brush the loose strands of hair from her face, Laura kissed her, inhaling a draught of sweet and milky innocence, before leaving her in the charge of her stuffed protectors.

Downstairs in the sunroom with the choice of a one hundred and eighty degree view, Laura stood at the window searching for signs of life over at Luther's home, half visible behind a stand of blackthorn, the flowers of which still held the glow of the day. A lamp was on in the living part of the house. His kitchen window reflected the sky. She was surprised to find herself waving, not understanding why. She felt warm and silly and let her arm fall back to her side, yet she stayed there, for a good while, hoping he was watching all the time; wanting to be watched. If he had seen her, did it look like a hello or a help? Was she the lady of the house or merely its captive? The structure felt huge around her.

She went into the snug and lay on the sofa.

They stopped in a column of full moon night that fell through the canopy like the devil's spotlight. The single torch they had between them appeared to provide little comfort and they clung to the perceived safety of this new and vague illumination, as if merely finding this spot in the darkness was a victory of sorts. Panting and holding on to each other, John was the first to get his breath back. Frank continued to breathe heavily, hands on his knees for support, until he vomited, emptying his night's drinks onto the track.

'You okay?'

'Yeah, much better, can't even feel my ankle. Ah fuck.' He lifted his foot out of the puddle of lager and partially digested meat. 'Please tell me we're almost out of here.'

'Can't be far now,' said John, patting Frank on the back.

They were nearly home. From where Luther had concealed himself, he could see around the corner, the exit, his home and the sheen of copper strips along the top of the new house. He took a lead pellet from his pocket and held it between his teeth, his face contorted into a demonic grin as he cocked the rifle. He loaded it and waited. He'd paralleled their walk home through the trees, staying out of sight yet making no attempt to keep quiet, snapping branches, activating an ancient gin-trap, listening to them squeal at the fierce metallic clap of its jaws, their stumbling run that took them across his trip wire, falling into stagnant stench, scrambling to retrieve their torch. He wished he'd had more time.

'You think it's him, really?'

'I fucking know it,' said John, 'he's got it in for me.'

'Hey, less of the victim, come on. What's your plan?'

'Beat him.'

'Fucking A.'

John swung the torch around, too erratic and rushed to be of any real use as a searchlight, but Luther crouched lower nonetheless.

'Where the fuck is he?'

Frank started laughing to himself, bent double, whilst coughing and spitting the last of his sick out.

'He's good though, isn't he? Look at us.'

'Well,' said John, finding some humour in the situation, 'I think we did some of it to ourselves; can't blame the hillbilly for everything.'

'Hillbilly's fucking right. He's probably spent his life catching what he eats and fucks.'

'True.'

'Probably has a favourite backwoods retard who obliges him.'

'Sucks her thumb and calls him daddy.'

'Touch of a good woman might civilise the cunt.'

Luther raised the air rifle and took aim.

John unzipped, pissed where he stood, put it away, wiped his hands on his trousers and pulled Frank upright.

'Come on,' he said.

The pellet hit him in the thigh. The yelp was followed by a drunken dash for safety.

It was seconds before they snagged his second trip wire, two lengths of fishing line stretched separately across their path. One was tied around the trigger of his loaded shotgun, its stock jammed into a nearby root system, the other around the makeshift peg securing a restrained lower bough. They screamed like children. The flash of orange had barely registered before the ear sucking explosion of both barrels woke every living creature they hadn't already disturbed. They were still screaming as the peg popped and the bough reasserted itself, sweeping through its dark kingdom at eye level like a medieval weapon, knocking them off their feet. The sounds of shock and fear faded as Luther ducked instinctively between the pines, through the bark of the fox and the clacking of the chickens, the squeal of pigs and the premature chorus of the birds, back to his home, to wait.

Luther slipped his shirt off in the dark, unable to remember the last time he had been audibly happy. The physical strangeness of the laugh and the realisation that it may have been his last one saddened him a little. He listened to the room in the hope a trace would remain, a reminder of what he had sounded like, but it was gone, just bare walls and the scuffing of his boot soles. The more he concentrated the more she came back and the memory of her joy brought him none. He dropped his shirt over the chair-back, covering Laura's cardigan, sat on his chair and undid his laces.

He was barefoot before the outrage began. Howls of

abuse, threats and injustice thrown at his home, drink-addled and vehement. A sly grin spread as Luther poured a bumper of whisky, swirling a mouthful around before scorching his gullet. Popping the button of his combats as he stood, he let them fall to the floor and stepped out of them, naked. One more mouthful; the flick of a switch, a grip on the handle, the straightening of his face, before he opened the door and stood framed with the light behind him.

'What's all the noise?'

John stopped his shouting. His head jutted forward as he scrunched his eyes to see.

'Don't be cute, Luther, I know it was you.'

'What was me?'

'That stuff,' he said, flinging his hand out to point back to where they had been, 'the guns and booby traps, I fucking know it was you.' He jabbed a drunken hand at Luther, but couldn't hold it still.

Luther stepped off his front porch and walked down the path to the two men standing at his gate. As he came out of silhouette, Frank put his hands over his face to hide his laughter. John was confused. He glanced at Luther's cock.

'Luther, you've got no clothes on.'

Frank's sniggering leaked between his fingers. Averting his gaze, John used every muscle available to his face to stop himself doing the same.

'It's warm. I was in bed. It was your gun that woke me up.'

'My gun?' Finding that serious form of sobriety that only the drunk can possess, John turned to Luther and held firm eye contact. 'You know that's not the truth.'

'Look at me.' Luther held his arms out. 'I've got nothing to lose.'

'Luther,' said John, stepping closer, adopting a conciliatory tone, 'why can't we just be neighbours?'

'We are. That's the problem; your problem.'

Although they still stared at each other, the finality of this comment and the threat it contained ended the altercation. Frank sensed this and pulled John away.

'Come on, John. He's not listening.'

John snatched his arm away.

'Fuck off, Frank, I'll leave when I'm ready. Me; not you, not him.'

Luther knew that John probably wouldn't remember the details in the morning, but he would never let go of the hate that was in the black of his eyes at that moment. It looked to be the only thing keeping him upright. When John decided he was ready, he snorted and gave a toss of his head for some imagined victory.

'Arsehole.'

He slumped away, shoulders first until he collided with Frank, who wrapped his arm around him with 'good for you' comfort and quickly made light of the situation in a conspiracy of cackling.

'Night then.'

Luther scratched his balls, pleased with his night's work.

Laura threw the quilt back and got up. She had been awake for hours, squeezing John's nose, turning him over, pinching him, punching him, putting pillows over his and her heads, anything to stop the snoring; all to no avail. Defeated, she left the room. Outside, Frank was no better, worse even. His door was wide open and he was lying on his back on top of the bed, naked and erect. Thank God Molly had slept right through most of it. Their snoring echoed around the landing, even after she closed both bedroom doors.

Laura had decided it was time for bed when she realised she wasn't going to find out what had gone on. What the loud bang that took her to the window was; why they were both filthy; why Luther had been standing naked in front of them both. Whatever it was hadn't been friendly, the way she'd seen John tear his arm from Frank's grip. They weren't ready to share it. They'd rediscovered some of their childish camaraderie by the time they fell into the house, even though she sensed it was edged with tension, and spent the best part of an hour and another bottle of wine hooting and howling like a pair of wanking chimps at each other's 'squeal piggy' backwoods jokes. Sitting at the breakfast counter, Frank had devoured most of the grilled cheese on toast she'd made, before insisting John perform 'Duelling Banjos' with him, without a banjo in sight. John's eye had been twitching, the way it always did when he was drunk and tired, but he agreed to the duet. She got up when he took his banjo out of its case and asked Frank what key they were playing in. It was too much. She declared she'd had enough. She'd cringed when Frank had wrapped his arm around her waist as she tried to leave, half a hand slipping beneath her top, and promised her they'd be good boys. John had nodded in agreement, eyes closed, head tilted as he turned his fingers in mid-air, tuning his instrument. She knew better.

'You won't,' she'd replied, hoping her smile showed tolerance and understanding, even appreciation of their behaviour. 'Besides, somebody has to be in a fit state to look after Molly. Either of you want to get up early?'

That ended their resistance and Frank, drawing his fingertips across the small of her back, allowed her to escape. Frank's fingers were never still. She often felt that there was an assumption, an implied shared fraternal ownership that John either didn't notice or didn't mind.

There'd been the pop of another bottle being uncorked as she walked through the sunroom. Luther's light had still been on when she'd climbed the stairs.

She took the long way around to Milton, trying to think of something to do or buy as she drove; a reason that would keep her out longer than it would take her to do the bottles. She enjoyed the journey, telling Molly the names of the plants and birds that she knew. At the recycling point she let the tailgate down and backed the truck right up to the bottle bank. Standing on the tailgate, Molly could reach the opening and help. They were halfway through smashing glass together when the reason pulled up beside them in a silver Jaguar.

'Mrs Payne.'

Cargill sat in his car, the window down, dressed in Sunday casuals wearing what looked to be Ray Ban Aviators. They didn't suit him. Laura didn't think the smile was sincere and was not inclined to respond. He took his glasses off and lost the smile.

'I'm sorry, I know how you must feel.'

'I don't think you do, Mr Cargill.'

Molly wasn't interested in Cargill and another bottle smashed as he turned his engine off, opened the door and climbed out of the air conditioning. Standing across the tailgate from Laura, they both watched as Molly finished the job, leaning right into the box to get the final bottle, a champagne magnum that Frank had brought. She had to hold it with both hands in order to lift it out and Laura helped her raise it to the opening. She giggled as the dregs dribbled down her arm from the upturned bottle. She let go and beamed, so obviously satisfied was she with the solid crunch of breaking glass.

'Finish.'

'Good girl,' said Laura, holding her arms out for a cuddle. With Molly in her arms she faced Cargill. 'You have something else to say?'

'Mrs Payne, you came to me and dealt with me in good faith. I did not reciprocate. It was not proper business or a decent way to behave, particularly towards somebody who was moving into our community. You have every right to be angry.'

'Betrayed, deceived, hoodwinked, exploited; made a fool of. I could go on.'

'It was never my intention to make a fool of you, or J.P. Listen, I don't feel good about the way things have gone. I was on my way out to see you when, well, I saw you. Would you come and have a coffee with me? I think if we talk about Luther you might understand. There's more that I should tell you.'

She didn't respond immediately, holding back.

'I'd like to hear.'

'Good. Here let me get that.' Molly climbed through to her child seat as he secured the tailgate and closed the truck door. 'It's been a while since I had a child seat, you okay to follow me?'

Cargill sat them at a simple wooden table to the side of the room and went to the bar. Molly stared through the window, mesmerised by the spokes of the waterwheel that gave the café its name. As they crept up the frame the spokes threw hypnotic shadows that swept across their table and over the other people in the café. Whether chatting, eating, drinking or reading alone, they all looked to be characters in a slow-moving, old-fashioned film. The wooden furniture in the Waterwheel Café looked to be refurbished or salvaged, a unity of design being achieved through paint. Bookshelves were dotted around the walls, between windows and doors, filling the spaces like wallpaper. Continuing this bookish theme, and what Laura liked most, was that each table was glass-topped, under which was a table-sized print of a page from a book. Looking round it seemed none of these pages had their parent book titles at the top. They were snatches of the story, a hint of what was. Reading the adjoining table, she was trying to work out if these pages had been picked at random, or if they had something that connected them, when Cargill arrived back.

'Here we go,' he said, placing three drinks on the table, 'one black coffee for mum and for mummy's helper, an orange juice, still in the bottle so we don't spill it, with a pink straw. You like pink?' Molly nodded and took the juice, not taking her eyes off Cargill. 'Pink okay with you, Mrs Payne?

'Pink's fine,' she said, 'thank you. What do we say, Molly?'

'Kyou.'

'My pleasure. And a cheeky wee cappuccino for me.'

Cargill sat opposite her. Much as she wanted to be angry, Laura found herself warming to him. His manner with Molly was easy and natural. It was obvious he was a dad, maybe even a granddad. Although she hoped she wasn't being fooled, she also thought that he was genuinely sorry about what he'd done, or failed to do. It was only the second time she'd met him, the first time she'd been able to get a word in edgeways.

'It's nice,' said Laura, 'the café. Not what I expected. I thought it would be a bit, well, you know, tacky, like Pitlochry; all dusty tartan and Scotty dog motifs.'

'Well, I'm glad we're able to confound your expectations. We're after more than the blue rinse pound and the one visit dollar.'

She smirked at the phrase.

'Are they for sale?' she said, pointing to the nearest shelf of paperbacks.

'Absolutely, we need to maximise our income. Monetise the space, as they say. Though you can part-pay with a book, if you like. A good book can make a difference to your bill.'

'Mills and Boon?'

'We send them to Pitlochry.'

He slurped from his cappuccino, licking the milk moustache away as he opened the wrapper on his little biscuit. He cast his eye over the clientele.

'I think it's why people come back,' he said. 'It's a real village. All these people live here, still would if the tourists stopped coming, touch wood.' He tapped the side of the table. 'In a way, it's kind of why I was coming out to see you. I meant what I said abut the community, you coming into it. You'll be shopping here, having coffees maybe, she'll be going to school. None of that crossed my mind until yesterday, when I realised you lived here. You stopped being the rich people who were building a big house. You became neighbours. Well, Luther's neighbours.'

'Do you need to make it sound so ominous? He's part of your community as well, isn't he?'

Cargill took a moment, another gulp, winked at Molly, who grinned back with the straw held between her front teeth.

'On the edge of, if at all,' he said. 'However, there's something you need to understand.' He realised that he was pointing at Laura. He put his hands up and sat back, sighing, annoyed with himself. 'I'm sorry; that was rude. You're not here to be lectured.'

'Accepted. Go on.'

'I don't mean to tell you what to do. But it would help if you understood why it is that the people of Milton, of a certain generation, more than tolerate Luther. There's even a warped sense of pride in him still being here. It takes a few years but his belligerence does become funny, honestly. How we laugh as we drive all the way around the valley instead of cutting up through the back of the church,' he said, without smiling.

'It is a long way, I suppose.'

'We're used to it.'

He leant forward and used a finger to draw a stick man amongst the sugar Molly had spilled from the pourer. Molly considered the figure before drawing her finger through his lines, wrecking the man. She then followed Cargill's lead as he showed her how to dab her finger on her tongue to wet it before pressing into the sugar to lift the crystals up so she could taste them. It was a sweet and sticky revelation. 'Mmm.' The look on her face meant he had a friend for life.

'Truth being told, Mrs Payne, Luther hasn't really been part of the village since Ishbel died.'

The viscous bitterness of cooling coffee coated her tongue, unpleasant to taste and swallow. Placing her cup in its saucer and pushing them away, she opened her biscuit and handed it to Molly to distract her from the sugar. Cargill used his napkin to sweep the sugar into his empty cup.

'I take it you didn't even know that.'

She shook her head. The coffee had been a bad idea; on top of the one she'd had this morning and without food, it burned her stomach, reminding her of the pain she used to get with ulcers.

'His mind snapped. It's taken him a long time to get back to where he is now, wherever that is.'

'He didn't say,' she said, regretting it immediately. She began re-running their meeting, trying to recall a wedding ring on his hand.

'You've spoken with Luther?'

Laura nodded. Cargill didn't have to ask. She could see he wanted to know more.

'Yesterday,' she said. 'He invited me in. He said I should see his home, seeing as he'd seen mine. But you would know all about that, right?'

She didn't intend it to come out so sharply. Cargill either didn't get the jibe or chose to ignore it, which she was grateful for.

'How was he?' he asked.

'Not unpleasant. Intense. I don't think he gets many visitors.'

Cargill's private smile was heavy with history and he could easily have made Laura feel small.

'He doesn't get any.' He studied her for a moment. 'I bet he was surprised to see you standing there. Did you have your hair up like that?'

'Does it matter?'

'Not to me, Mrs Payne. It would just make sense, that's all; the likeness is uncanny. Do you know I've never been inside his home since she died? I tell you that for illustration. I have managed that man's financial affairs for the last sixteen years and I have no idea how he lives.'

'Frugally – from what I saw.'

'That does not surprise me in the least. He is nothing if not contrary.'

Cargill continued looking at her, shaking his head, slowly, with a smile on his face that was starting to annoy her.

'What happened?'

He became solemn, placed his fingertips together forming a basket of thought with his hands and took a breath.

'She drowned, in the lochan, the one you now own.'

Laura felt sick.

'How old was she?'

'Little bit older than this one,' he said, stroking the back of Molly's hand with his finger, 'four or five.'

'Oh my God,' said Laura covering her mouth. 'It was his daughter.'

'Late summer; it was still warm. She'd just started school, same class as my eldest. She's at the university now. It really does feel like yesterday.'

'That's awful.'

'Awful isn't close. He carried her coffin out of the church on his own; walked to the cemetery with her, crying all the way, talking to her as though she needed his comfort. At the grave…' The words caught in his throat and Cargill had to hold his breath, steady his breathing. His eyes filled. 'Well, at the grave he wouldn't let go. His arms were like steel bands, holding her to his chest. I think he would have crushed the child in her box if it hadn't been for Tarragh. She peeled his fingers away, begged him to let her help. When they came away, she took hold of them and all he said was 'God help me.' The only time I ever heard him ask for help. They lowered her in together. He filled the grave. They walked home together. No help from, and not a word to, anybody else. Precious few since.'

It could have been the way Laura rubbed the sugar from Molly's fingers. The heavy silence that appeared between Mummy and the man, the way Laura ran her hand over Molly's face, holding her for a long time. Intuitively, Molly sensed something had changed, for the worse. The day of sugar and biscuits was over. She lost confidence in her own happiness and held her arms out. Laura wrapped both arms around Molly as she lifted her from the baby chair.

'I should get her home, clean her properly.'

'Sure. Here let me get the door for you.' Cargill continued talking as he walked with Laura to the door. 'There's more to tell, and know, about Luther, but that loss is all that really matters. There was a time we didn't think he'd carry on, if you know what I mean.'

Cargill opened the door and stood aside, gesturing for Laura to leave first. She waited for him outside, assuming he would be following.

'No, you go on Mrs Payne. I'll just settle the bill. I'll see you again no doubt, now we're neighbours. Be happy to talk to you anytime.'

'Mr Cargill.'

The drop of his shoulders said he knew what was coming. She didn't need to ask.

'She left,' he said, 'as suddenly as she'd arrived, which was typical.'

'How?'

'She was a free spirit, Mrs Payne. Unpredictable: in an attractive way. There was nothing tied down about her, if you know what I mean. She was exciting.'

'You liked her?'

'Everybody did.' Cargill looked away. 'Anyway, she left. It's not uncommon, apparently. Few couples survive that kind of trauma.'

'Was it his fault?'

'No, but he shouldered it.'

With that he held his wallet up to remind her he had to pay and let the door close.

Laura had Molly in the car and the engine running by the time Cargill came out from The Waterwheel. He gestured, indicating for her to wait. When it was apparent he was coming over to her she let the window down, curious to hear what else he had to say.

'Do you want me to tell you why he let you in? He thought she'd come back.'

'I'm sorry?'

'If you'll follow me to my house I'll show you what I mean.'

'Molly's due a change. Will it take long?'

'It needn't.'

'Okay,' she said.

She reversed out of the parking space and followed Cargill to his home on the outskirts of Milton, overlooking the golf course.

Luther had watched her leave that morning. He'd been waiting. She had a dress on today, bright and summery; the cotton clung to her. The early sun had cut through the cotton to show her shape as she'd loaded a box of bottles into the back of the truck. It was a familiar shape, one he had known, coveted and missed.

She had troubled his sleep, illuminating labyrinthine corridors, cobwebbed and without footprint, opening sealed doors leading back to memories consciously avoided and images long dismissed from his dreams. She reached into him. There was no keeping her out or controlling what she released. She was seeping through the plates of his armour. After being screwed down tight for so long he could feel them loosening, threads unwinding.

Laura pulled into the drive in time to see John and Frank running along the boardwalk in the scud. At the end they did a full-on leap into the water, their tackle on display. She knew they had timed it for her to see. It was the kind of shit Frank always got John up to.

As Laura opened the door Molly was craning her neck to watch the pair of them splashing each other. She took her sugary hand out of her mouth and pointed.

'Mummy, daddy swimming, daddy swimming.'

'So I see.'

Laura lifted her out and put her down.

'You want to go and see daddy swimming?'

Molly looked at the boardwalk and then looked back to Laura.

'It's okay, daddy won't shout. I'll come with you, come on.'

As she took Molly's hand, Laura noticed an empty bottle of champagne on the barbeque alongside a carton of orange juice.

By the time mother and daughter stood over the water, John was pulling long broad breast-strokes across the middle of the lochan, cutting through the surface, his head ducking with each forward thrust. Frank was closer to the boardwalk, sculling through the shallows on his back, eyes closed; his bobbing cock keeping speed with his head like a duckling in tail of its mother.

'You want to put that away?' said Laura, 'Some of us haven't eaten.'

'Hey,' he smirked, 'there's girls the world over crying out for Little Frank.'

'It doesn't look like there's a lot to cry about from here, and the cold water's not doing him any favours either.'

Frank sniggered as he rolled onto his front, spun a somersault to give his backside and bollocks an airing and set off after John.

'How much have you had this morning?'

'A couple of Bucks Fizz,' he said, 'to take the edge off.'

'You sure you're okay to be swimming?'

He didn't answer. As good a swimmer as John was, Frank's front crawl sliced away at the distance between them and he reached the far end at the same time, pushing John's head under for good measure.

Laura sat on the boardwalk edge with Molly, leaning forward over dangling feet, waving at each other's reflections. In the brief mirror-perfect moment that the lochan offered she saw Molly waving goodbye, her reflection as far below the surface as they were above it.

When John and Frank returned, Laura had her arm around Molly, tears running down her face.

'Hey, what's the matter,' John said, treading water.

'Nothing. I'm,' she waved their concern away, 'I'll tell you later. You need towels?'

'That would be good.'

Laura stood and took hold of Molly's hand to help her up.

'Leave her with us,' said Frank, 'she'll be okay.'

'No, I'll take her.'

'Laura,' said John, 'we're here, she'll be fine.' He flicked droplets at Molly, who squealed and waved her free hand in an attempt to stop them hitting her. 'Is this about the other day?'

Laura almost found a smile for his attempt to understand.

'Yes, but not how you mean. I'll get the towels. Watch her.'

She let go of Molly, enabling her to use both hands to bat away the flicks of water from daddy and Uncle Frank. Her delight escalated the closer Laura got to the house, and knowing they would go too far, she was already picturing Molly's change of clothes.

There was no splash. Molly's scream had nothing to do with water. It was terror and pain. Her arms flailed about her as though she was beating away the devil himself. Hearing mummy call she ran down the boardwalk to Laura faster than she had ever moved, mouth stretched open, eyes bulging, her forearm already swelling. The two bee stings were still in her arm. Her screaming escalated as Laura scratched them out, hysterical as she was scooped up and carried to the truck.

'Laura, wait for me.'

Laura saw John climbing the ladder from the lochan, running towards them. She didn't even bother to argue with him, climbing in and speeding out of the drive spitting gravel backwards leaving deep ruts in her wake, a wet, naked husband in her rear-view mirror.

Barrelling through the trees saved time but concentrated panic. The crack and scrape of branches along the bodywork and the bouncing of the truck as it pummelled new ruts created its own anxiety. Molly screamed all the way to Milton. By the time Laura whipped her from the back seat and ran into the surgery, she was too upset to say or do anything when she saw Luther's Defender alongside the building, its back door open.

When Dr Ali Shah took the ice pack off Molly's arm, the swelling had gone down enough for Laura to believe his reassurances. His voice was a cure. Even Molly had calmed as he spoke to her, oblivious to her crying, confident she could hear, that he was getting through. Though the information was for Laura's benefit, Molly was lulled by the measured tone it was delivered in.

'There you go now, coming down nicely. I think maybe because you had two bee stings close together, this was why the reaction was so bad. I don't think you are allergic; however, you will need to be careful, trying not to get stung would be best don't you think? Is Molly allowed a sweetie now, for being brave? Sugar free and no gelatine, how does that sound to mum?'

'That sounds lovely, thank you.'

'No need to thank me,' he said, sliding his glasses back up the bridge of his nose with his middle finger. 'What kind of doctor doesn't have sweeties, hey?' He took a white plastic container from his top drawer. 'Especially a doctor with a sweet tooth.' He pulled the blue lid off the box and held it out for Molly to choose one. She glanced to Laura who nodded okay.

'It might be worth speaking to your neighbour, don't you think? He, I know, does not get stung. There may be a secret to this.'

'He was outside when...' Laura stopped. 'Was Luther here to see you?'

'He was.'

'Is he okay?'

'How many people come to see a doctor because they feel okay?

'I suppose.' She declined a sweet. 'Nothing serious though?'

'Doctor-patient confidentiality precludes me from answering that, Mrs Payne. But he is not being as, how do you say, cooperative or optimistic, as I would hope. Anyway, you should ask him about bees.'

He held out the box for Molly to take one more.

Outside the surgery, Luther's Defender was now parked next to Laura's truck. The rear door was still open. Luther sat inside with his feet on the step, his head between his knees. He was coughing. Laura waited for him to finish before she went over, wanting him to hear what she had to say. Each dry bark caused him to tighten in on himself, at one point almost losing his balance, only catching himself at the last moment. She stood there until the coughing stopped. It was long enough to notice just how overwhelming their truck was alongside all the other vehicles in the car park. Luther's was battered but looked stubborn and indestructible, function over form in every sense. She was beginning to feel awkward, an unwelcome spectator, when he finally howked the last bit up, followed by a spit and a groan. When he raised his head Laura could see his eyes were watering and he was red with the exertion. He flicked most of a cigarette away.

'Are you okay?' she said.

He nodded. 'Won't be doing that again.'

'Well done you,' said Laura, grinding the cigarette out. 'It's never too late.'

He snorted.

'I stopped smoking twenty-five years ago.'

'So what was that?'

'Thought I'd give it a go again, see if I still liked it.'

'Beeman,' said Molly, pointing at Luther. 'Beeman.'

Luther, noticing that Molly had remembered his name, slid from the Defender and dropped down onto one knee, so that his head was level with hers, in her world.

'And how are you, Molly?'

'Sore.' Molly held her arm out for Luther to see. 'Sore.'

He saw the swelling and took hold of her arm. Laura watched as he turned it, serious, inspecting, to see how many stings there were. He stroked one of the stings.

'Sore?'

Molly nodded.

He kept hold of her arm for a few seconds before standing and putting his hand deep into one of the side pockets of his gilet. He leant to give a small, metal tube of toothpaste to Molly. She looked at it and then at Luther. She was about to put it to her mouth when Luther got back down on his knee to explain.

'No no, it's not to eat.' He tapped the tube in her grip,

'Toothpaste. If you get stung again, put toothpaste on it,' he made a rubbing motion just above one of the stings, glanced up at Laura, 'it will help, as good as anything else.'

'It might help even more if you were to say you're sorry, to her at least? Don't you think you owe her that? Didn't you hear her when I took her in there? She was terrified.'

Luther looked genuinely confused by Laura's suggestion.

'I didn't sting her.'

'But Luther, they were your bees. You're the beeman.'

'Bees fly. Bees sting. I can't apologise for that, or them.'

'Well – why are you here? Why were you waiting? I thought you'd heard her crying and...'

'To see you.' He leant back against his vehicle as though he needed the support. 'I wanted to see you again. And her. If I say I'm sorry to her she'll think it was my fault.'

'Luther!'

'What?'

'Don't you think she associates it with you already? She showed you her arm.'

'I hope not.' He placed his hand on Molly's head. 'I don't want a girl like her to think anything bad was my fault.'

She saw him swallow as he gazed at the little girl spreading toothpaste on her arm, and she knew he was looking at Ishbel.

She closed her eyes. She could feel her anger dissipating.

'It was only a bee sting.'

He looked at Laura.

'Dress her in plain clothes,' he said, 'you as well, I would say. Something pale, neutral; bright colours attract them.' He gestured to the print on Laura's dress, pointing to the individual colours as he spoke. 'They think you're flowers; gorse, broom, hawthorn, blackthorn, rape, wild cherry. And don't wave your arms about when there's a bee close by, that just aggravates them; try and stay still, cover your face. If there's more than one; run away.' He closed the rear door. 'Stay clean. It could help, but it's no guarantee.'

She took Molly's hand and followed Luther as he climbed into the driver's seat.

'Luther.'

He waited while she chose her words.

'It doesn't have to be now, but if you ever want to talk about anything else, anything.'

'What do you have in mind?'

There was a smirk, almost; a hint of knowing. It was a challenge for her to come out with it, tell him what she thought she knew. Laura wasn't sure if he was teasing her again, or if he wanted to know what she had found out in the village in her short time here. She took her time and let him feed off the sight of her while he waited for a response. The curiosity was gone. Maybe he was noticing the differences between her and Tarragh. She saw admiration, appreciation, something that convinced her he was looking at Laura Payne. It was a good feeling. She went to touch him but lost courage and her hand hung between them for him to take, but he didn't.

'I know why you stare at me,' she said.

His eyes were small blue storms; mostly rain, no thunder, some lightning.

'Do you now?'

Luther pulled the cellar door closed behind him and secured it from the inside. Downstairs, he hauled the stack of empty potato boxes away from the wall. In doing so, he exposed the sheet of plywood. Painted the same white as the walls, with an ad hoc rope handle, it was wedged into the rough gap between the two worktops. It was further secured with wooden wedges driven in either side. He gave the handle a pull. There was no give whatsoever. At the bottom he could see a buckle in the wood which had resulted from his determination to get it to fit. There were still dents where he had kicked the board until it submitted to the space. Running a finger across the top he felt the cold of the air that left the cellar through the gap, the breeze that had chilled Laura.

Taking a mallet from the tool-rack he knocked out the four side wedges. He pulled against the rope but the makeshift door was still jammed tight. Forcing his fingers through the top gap he used his strength and body weight to prise it away from the wall. Once there was sufficient space to fit an axe handle in, it was a matter of leverage and seconds before he saw the plywood pop out and he could drag it away from the entrance.

The chisel marks in the stone doorway appeared as fresh as the day they had been made; a rough and unskilled chipping at rock that had been in the way. He recalled being brought down here by Old Callum, just before he was moved away to be closer to his daughter who was going to look after him. Callum had lived alone for over thirty years and was not keen on leaving. More than that, he did not want the cavern to be abused.

'Take the left fork,' he had told Luther, pushing a torch into his hand, 'it'll be about ten minutes, I would say.'

Luther had no idea where the opening led to. He had been both curious and nervous.

'You're not coming?'

'Ach no, I have only one visit left in me. I think I will do it alone. No offence to you Luther, but,' he waved Luther into the passageway, 'go on, you'll understand.'

Callum's wrinkled face, half trust, half devilment, was intrigue enough for Luther to enter.

When Luther did return, almost an hour later, Callum had cackled with delight and relief as he'd emerged. The understanding must have been in his eyes.

'You're the piper,' said Luther.

'I was,' he said, 'for over twenty years. It's been some time since I played.'

'You leave them in there all the time?'

'It's where they belong. So then, Luther, I take it we have a deal?'

'We do.'

They shook hands.

Callum had poured whisky and told Luther how, when his girls had moved away and Mrs MacLeod had passed away, he had been in the cellar, where Mrs MacLeod had always refused to go due to its terrible chill, and he had put his arm through the crack in the rock.

'I couldn't say why. After about a foot, it widened out. I could wave my fingers, side to side. Well, at that moment I decided to find out how wide it got. I chipped away for two years until the crack was the man-sized opening it is now.'

'Two years?'

'Aye.'

'Callum,' said Luther. 'How long have you been on your own?'

'A long time.' Callum gestured to the gap in the rock. 'That was my lifeline. Do you understand?'

'I think so.'

'The first time I went through, I took my hammer and chisel with me, expecting more to be done. But it just went on, a narrow tunnel, rising for most of the way, then dropping a wee bit into,' he smiled, 'well, you've seen.'

'I have.'

'I believe I was the only human being to have ever set foot in that cave. You're the second. Think about that, Luther, more people have been on the moon.'

Old Callum was moved away and died soon after.

The cavern became Luther's.

It was three years later that he took her for the first time, creeping through behind him, hands on his shoulders, following the beam from a single torch. He had known her for just under a year. Her response to the cavern consolidated every love and hope he had pinned on her, on them. It became their place; the secret of it a conspiracy between them. When he told her that more people had walked on the moon, she took her shoes off and tried to cover every inch of the cavern floor so that she would always be the first, at least one place on the earth, 'or in the earth,' she had joked. This notion faded the more time she spent in the cave. She claimed to have felt things, mostly good. She became convinced they were sharing the chamber with those that left no footprints; that it was a junction, an invisible kissing gate. The first time they made love in the cave she had held his face against hers, eyes almost touching and told him, 'It's a baby girl, her name is Ishbel.' Nine months later, Ishbel spent her first night swaddled between her parents in the place that she was conceived. Exhausted mother had curled around their daughter and joined her in sleep in the shallow stone hollow that they called the bed. Luther had gazed upon them for hours, thankful that, after many solitary years, they had finally happened to him. He had cried for the first time since he had been a schoolchild. When Ishbel woke for milk and Tarragh stirred in response, Luther had moved away to wipe his face and feed the fire, its smoke twisting upwards and across to the vertical fissure in the cave wall that Old Callum had called the chimney. As he watched her suckle, it felt to him that the cave was the glowing nucleus of his world and that everything forever would revolve around this mother and child.

Luther still kept this orbit. He held on to what had been.

On Tarragh's twenty-eighth birthday he had placed tin foil tea light candles the length of the passageway and placed flowers on the swept smooth floor to be crushed by her bare feet. He could still recall the smell as he had floated in her wake, introducing summer to the underworld. Ishbel's first steps through the passageway had been curious yet without fear. She had been carried there countless times and knew the purpose of her walk. Luther and Tarragh had cajoled, cheered, walked backwards to lead her and lifted her high when she had made it. They thought to make handprints, as if in some ancient refuge with nebulous thoughts of future existence but ended up with body prints, stark outlines against the wall of a mother standing alongside her child. The impression was precise and finessed by the artist, who knew the curl of the hair, the bow of the unsure gait, the upward gaze and the downward glance. His stencilled hands were the signature beside them.

He looked at the back of his arms, recalling how much of the claymix Ishbel had managed to spread over him instead of the wall. He remembered splashing with Tarragh and Ishbel as he washed it off, chipping it from his arm hairs, fingernailing it from the creases in the back of his knuckles, the dark moons of his nails submerged in the bowl of ochrous water. He could feel their hands, soft and squidgy within his grip, smooth and slender around his wrists, as they stood either side of him, one on an upturned tin bucket. He felt weakened by her return. Tarragh had been so much with him over the last two days that it seemed she was by his side now as he walked to their place. It was a journey Luther never thought he would retake.

Waking one morning, in the bad times after Ishbel, she hadn't been there. Her shoes were by their bed. He'd found her body in the cavern. Lying where she had lain the first night of Ishbel's life, clutching a child-sized bundle of blanket to her chest. The rock floor beneath her head was stained with tears, salt white at the drying edges. He had sat her up, wrapping her tight in her favourite rug so that only her face showed and kept vigil while she cooled and his mind boiled. He had banished all memories of leaving her, of boarding the passage up or the next year of his life.

At the fork on the passage Luther noticed a rillet of water running out of the left and down into the right. Long ago, when Luther had asked where the right fork went, Callum told him he had never found out.

'It goes on forever, I would say.' Sadness had troubled Callum's face. 'My Bheag is down there somewhere. I shouted after her but she was exploring. By the time she started with her barking it was already too late, she was lost. Her barking got fainter, even as I went after her myself, but the right fork splits and it drops and there is rockfall and underground pools and gaps too small for an old man to follow. I had to come back. I couldn't help her.'

The idea of the lost dog had stayed with Luther. The thought of her in the pitch black, yelping as she bumped off the sharp walls, stumbling blindly for days, deeper into the cave system until she came to a dead end, cold, hungry, whimpering and exhausted, to lie down and wait for Callum or death.

Luther continued up the left fork which was damp underfoot. He hoped the cavern hadn't flooded. At the highest point, just before the drop into the cavern, Luther could hear running water, the stream above him. In the past this had only been possible when it was in full flow. There was a gash of daylight where the stream had eroded its bank, exposing a split in the bedrock. The summer flow produced a trickle; enough to maintain a modest display of lime green fern fronds growing from the cave wall, adjacent to the light. He imagined that in the winter, water must pour through; flooding into the right passage, not stopping until it washed over Bheag's bones. Luther jammed his handkerchief into the narrow end of the gash to help him identify it above ground, not certain what he would do with this knowledge.

He was relieved to see the ground beyond him dry and untouched. He narrowed the focus of his head, torch to minimise peripheral light in an attempt to control what he saw and when he saw it. The irrational hope that she wouldn't be there had all but gone.

The cavern had changed. There was no way of knowing if he'd applied the change. He had determined to find old Callum's pipes, the firepit, the stone bowl where they had slept, the wall paintings, all the things that were not her. But as he stood in the entrance, the pencil of light crept across the floor. His legs trembled. He leant against the curved wall before they gave way.

Her fleshless feet stuck out from the rug. His mouth dried. The air had always been cool and fresh, pulled as it was through the front door of Luther's house and never allowed to rest until it slipped out of the cavern's chimney in a continuous cycle of renewal. It now carried the tongue-shrinking tang of calcium, as if it had been filtered through her. The pattern of the Navajo rug was dull and stained. It was one of her few possessions when they had met, pulled from the ashes of an earlier relationship as the only thing worth salvaging. He had never asked who had wrapped her in it first. It now lacked content. It had sagged into folds of collapse and subsidence, not warmth or comfort. He closed his eyes and hunkered down, pushing hard against the rock to feel real pain. He had to steady himself. The more he tried to see Tarragh as she was, the more he saw Laura, and he didn't want her here. He knew the difference. He knew, he knew the difference.

He started again.

Her feet weren't fleshless. Skin had dried and shrunk back from the nails, wrapping around the bones and joints like bark on a winter sleeper, leaving toes like brittle kindling. Knowing that he could spend the rest of his life trying to imagine what she would look like, he looked at her. His chest contracted, enslaved once again. His breathing was stilled by his disbelief.

'Tarragh.'

It was her face. Old love hit him like a landslide. There

was no horror. She was there.

Luther knelt next to Tarragh, dizzy with memory, close to happy. Her hair, parted down the centre, was swept either side of her face into the loose ponytail he knew to be behind her. Her eyes were closed as though in serene contemplation. The parchment-dry skin that was preserved taut across her high cheekbones sank where her cheeks would be, more concave than he remembered, giving an impression of what she would have looked like if she had aged. He knew he could have loved her forever. Her lips were slightly parted in a smile of what looked to him to be peace or satisfaction. He was no longer angry with her. He was envious. He had always understood that it wasn't a matter of dying but a need to be released from the pain. His pain lay in the distance she had created between them in order to do this. She didn't let him back in. She wouldn't let him help. He stroked her face.

'I knew you hadn't come back.' He sighed and closed his eyes against the burning sensation of tears. 'I wanted it to be you.'

He moved the light away. There was a flash from Old Callum's pipes. He walked towards them.

He ran his fingers over the silver ferrule of the bass drone. Beneath the fine layer of dust they were untarnished. They sparkled. For the first time, he felt it was wrong that they were no longer played, that life should be breathed back into them.

The faint smell of ash from the fire pit, like church incense, was enough to warm him and bring to mind their underground feasts of venison on long skewers; salmon nailed to a thick board, oil sizzling as it roasted, fireside; potatoes baking in the embers alongside vegetables wrapped in foil with garlic and wild herbs.

He sat between the pipes and Tarragh, in the natural trough that swept across the floor, the rock worn smooth by an age-old watercourse that once ran through the cave when the chimney was a waterfall and the firepit a plunge pool. His back curled into the half-wave of the bank. His feet hung over the cusp of the opposite bank that dropped down to the entrance. Unwinding the focus of his torch, the light, softening as it spread, revealed the ghostly outlines and handprints of a lost family. Sweeping to his left, torch-light reflected back at him off the tin casings of countless tealights they had lit, wedged into the nooks and ledges of the wall alongside pieces of glass and mirror, masks made from cooking foil pressed onto their faces, a mobile made from bottle tops and beaten spoons, a tin can candelabra and myriad other shiny additions to the stone, her idea of subterranean starlight.

In their time, she'd turned their hideaway into a grotto. In the time since it had become a shrine.

He stayed for a long time, reacquainting himself with their secret place.

When he finally got to his feet, he spoke to her.

'It's so peaceful down here. I told myself that I wouldn't come back. I think I may have been wrong.'

Before he stepped back into the passageway, he turned back to Tarragh. The longer he stared at her, the easier it became to think of her apart from Laura.

'She has a little girl. Like we did.'

As the truck crunched down to the house John ran from the

sunroom and headed straight to the rear door. Before Laura had the brakes on, he had Molly unbuckled and hoisted out of her chair.

'Hey, how's my baby girl? Let daddy see.' He held her arm in his hand and pulled a face of cartoon pain. 'Ooh, that looks sore. Does it still hurt?'

Molly shook her head, curls swinging, and John laughed and hugged her tight, telling Frank what a brave daughter he had and thanked Laura for getting her to the doctor's so quickly in case it was something. But it was nothing, so everything was okay. Then they laughed at how ridiculous and pathetic they must have looked running along the boardwalk without any clothes on.

That's what should have happened.

She was surprised when they weren't there to meet them on their return. It was only as she was unbuckling her sleepy daughter from the seat that she saw John and Frank coming out of Luther's. She couldn't be sure if they were arguing but whatever it was, they stopped when they saw her. Luther's Defender was parked alongside his house and she hoped they hadn't done anything stupid. He'd been through enough. John had the decency to put some pace into his stride and he was keen to see his daughter.

'How is she?'

'She's fine,' said Laura, 'It was only a bee sting.'

'The fuck it was.'

The speed of his response and the flash of anger in his eye told Laura he wouldn't listen to any attempt to lessen the incident. He had been saving this up since she left. It was additional fuel.

'John, can you watch your language in front of Molly?'

'Fucker knows it's his fault. That's why he wouldn't come out of his cellar,' he said pointing back at Luther's. 'Locked himself in.'

'What's his fault?'

'Molly being stung, to start with.'

She saw her cardigan stuffed into John's pocket and knew what was coming, sooner or later, so she started to prepare.

'Bees fly, John, they sting. It happens. We need to be aware. It's a different set of dangers living here, that's all. They weren't sent – by anybody.'

'He can control them though, surely,' said Frank as he arrived.

'Don't be so stupid and don't try to wind him up.'

'I'm not. But I think he's playing with you,' said Frank, 'You know he is, John. He doesn't want you here.'

'Don't be so ridiculous,' she said.

'What's ridiculous? He's been rude, he's been obstructive and his bees stung little Molly. That's not a good start.'

'You've been here one day, Frank, how could you know anything?'

'Only one day less than you.'

'At least we've met the man.'

'Oh, we know that,' he said, smirking. 'We know that, don't we, John?'

'Frank. What are you so happy about?'

'Who said I was happy?'

'Listen,' she said, turning to John, not wanting to be provoked, 'I really can't be arsed with your stupid schoolboy games.'

John wasn't smiling. He reached into the huge side pocket of the combat shorts he was too old for and pulled out the cardigan, holding it in front of her like evidence.

'What's this all about?'

'Coffee,' she said. 'I spilled coffee and he was kind enough to wash it so it didn't stain.'

'Oh, really? What a lovely man,' said Frank, still trying to inject malice into the situation.

'Shut up,' she said. 'This has nothing to do with you.'

He shut up. But he didn't go away.

John still held the cardigan out. What did he want from her? She realised that he had nothing else to say. He'd been wound up tight by Frank. She was more than pissed off with John's suspicion and the implication it contained, but the fact that he was so malleable, so willing to be manipulated against her was what galled her. She snatched the cardigan, closed the gap between them and ignored Frank.

'I made a mistake. You said you'd dealt with it. If you're going to think I'm fucking every man I talk to, then maybe we should just call it a day now, because I'm not living like that.'

She turned to walk away but he gripped her and spun her back around. 'We're not calling anything a day. Not after what I've put into us.'

She recognised that last comment as John's voice and was at least grateful that he was thinking for himself again. Molly squirmed in the tension between them. Laura looked down at the fingers digging into her flesh, his hand clamping her to him.

'Let go,' she said.

It was as though he hadn't realised what he was doing. His features sagged, surrendered, as though seeing the force he exerted upon her shamed him. It was all she needed. As he released his grip she stretched up on her tiptoes to put her mouth to his ear. 'I don't need you. Don't make me not want you.' She looked him in the eye, gave his arm an affectionate squeeze that she hoped he understood and walked into the house wanting Frank to be gone, for John to come home.

STAY AWAY FROM *MY* WIFE. It was a rushed, capitalised scrawl across the open page of Luther's journal. It spoke more of desperation than anger and he was inclined to ignore it. But it was further evidence that John had been in his house, uninvited. The cellar door had been stuck and difficult to open. The outside showed signs of stamping and kicking. The handle was newly loose in its casing. Why? What had he wanted, seen, taken? The large elastic band still bound together the completed pages of the journal, so he hadn't read anything. A quick check confirmed that what little he possessed was still in its place. It was only when he sat down that Luther noticed her cardigan was missing. He almost smiled. John must have been surprised when he saw it hanging over the back of a stranger's chair, wondered how it got there. Did he think she took it off for Luther? That would be the start of the torment. There's no way out of doubt; not once it's set in.

John must have been brooding. Although there had been no letup in Frank's chat, she noticed that he wasn't really responding, at least not with his usual blind enthusiasm. In response to John's reluctance to interact, Frank became noticeably louder than usual and she knew it was for her benefit. He was annoyed that she'd taken his baby brother away from him. His play-pal wasn't in the playing mood and he was making sure she knew he blamed her. He avoided her, they both did, yet he made sure he could be heard, regardless of which room she was in. Laura was gratified to hear John defending her against some of Frank's accusations, however reasonable he tried to make them sound. Not once did she hear Frank say anything in her favour or agree with anything John said in her defence. She was sitting at the breakfast counter feeding Molly when she heard the word unfaithful come through the open windows of the sunroom. It was the third or fourth time he'd used it, like a lure on a barb, goading John into a response that Frank would finally find appropriate, like kicking her out, divorcing her, taking 'the kid' away from her. Why wouldn't he move on, or allow them to? He kept trying to drag John back to that one night. She didn't even revisit. She'd boxed away the guilt and moved on. John's telling Frank was as big a betrayal in her mind: and definitely a bigger mistake. Laura's hand trembled as she guided the spoon into Molly's mouth. Three fucking years and he was still at it.

It was John who brought it to an end. Her John.

'Frank, enough.'

'What?'

'Just give it a rest.'

'I was only…'

'I know.' She heard a chair scrape on the patio. 'I know what you're saying. Just don't say it again, please.'

In the peace that followed she imagined Frank sealing his lips, raising his eyebrows, putting his arms up halfway, part mock-acceptance, part, hey, I'm only trying to help.

She heard the door slide to, muting the sounds of the

outside.

John came into the kitchen and stood on the other side of Molly. He studied her arm as Laura tried to feed her.

'Stings are almost gone,' he said.

'I know.'

'Sore,' said Molly, prodding the pale swelling with her finger.

'Sore gone?'

She nodded. He kissed the stings.

'I'm sorry,' said John.

'About?'

'What I said, earlier on, the cardigan. It was a shitty thing to do.'

'It was.'

'And everything he's said since. I…'

'You can't apologise for him.'

'I may as well. He won't. Don't think he'll ever forgive you.'

She flung the plastic spoon into the sink. It clattered around the aluminium bowl as she wiped Molly's face with a tea-towel.

'He's got nothing to forgive me for. If you think he has, you can just go right back outside and sit with him.'

He sighed and sat down on one of the breakfast stools. He pulled the bow loose behind Molly's neck and took the bib away, rolling it into itself to catch all the bits. He handed it to Laura. She threw it straight into the washing machine.

'It's got nothing to do with him,' he said.

'So why do you listen?'

'I don't know.' He couldn't meet her stare. His head dropped, chin to chest, embarrassed as he thought it through like a pupil in the class spotlight trying to hide his face. 'I hardly ever see him; don't want to argue with him when I do.'

'You indulge him.'

'I know.'

'Seriously, you're like a pair of naughty toddlers, pushing the limits.'

'I don't want to lose him.'

'John. Where do you think he's going? He comes to see you: you, not us, every time a contract finishes. He needs you. I wish you could see that.'

'I do.' He smiled at Laura, 'There you go, I've said it. What's he got, apart from shitloads of money?'

'Nothing. His life is an empty room.'

She could tell that this truth didn't make John happy and regretted having said it with such satisfaction. She was about to try and make some kind of amends when he said, 'We're his family.' The words made her shiver from the top of her head through her heel and into the earth. The idea of a lifetime of 'Uncle Frank' and his visits didn't fill her with joy.

'He's got a drink problem,' she said. 'That's something.'

'Well, it's more than he had a moment ago, so let's not take it away, not just now.'

John took a bottle of white from the fridge, breaking the screw-top seal in the same motion, spinning the lid onto the counter, where it flipped upside down and rattled in ever decreasing circles until it settled. He held the wine up to Laura like a waiter would, as though to tempt her with the label.

'Okay.' She handed Molly to him. 'I'll be out. Just let me clean up. You could maybe clean the barbeque, get it going again. I'll make kebabs. They'll be ready by the time it's hot.'

'Sounds good,' he said.

She took her time in the kitchen. After mixing a marinade, into which she dropped the lamb she'd trimmed and cubed, she brushed, mopped and wiped every surface, allowing the meat ample time to tenderise and the flavours to marry. Once this was done she prepared the kebabs, alternating marinated lamb with red onion wedges, reserving the liquid for basting. When the dishwasher was full, the chopping board away, the knife wiped and in its rack and there was nothing else she could find to do, Laura took the kebabs out to the barbeque, the smell of which had already wound itself about her.

When Laura stepped out, it was as though she and John hadn't talked. He was listening to Frank, who was still going on about who was responsible for Molly's sting, where fault lay. John was sat in a chair with Molly on his knee while Frank tended the coals, drinking wine and waving the stainless steel utensils about as he spoke. John was nodding, as though he saw the logic in Frank's already half-cut arguments. The one she had walked into seemed to hinge on the fact that Luther, in harvesting the honey, would appear to be getting all the rewards whilst undertaking none of the responsibilities of controlling the bees, as though it was simply a matter of discipline.

'Hey, you know what else?' said Frank, stumbling across another path into an argument, 'I'm sure there's some kind of law that says you can't keep bees within so many metres of another house, or maybe any domestic residence, I'm not sure. You should look into that though, don't you think? Get him to move them, with the law on your side. He couldn't complain about that, could he?'

The goodness of the last hour dissipated.

'Frank,' she said, 'let's just let it go for now. Molly's fine, we know we need to be careful. Let's just eat, get her to her bed, it's past her bedtime already.'

'Well I have to say, Laura, you're taking this well, considering what he did to your daughter.'

'He didn't do anything.'

Frank furrowed his brow, a perplexed look on his face.

'Well he didn't. Molly was stung by bees, not by Luther. That's…' she paused and in the pause took pleasure in the anticipation of how they would both react, 'why he wouldn't apologise.'

John sat up, leant forward and made it clear with his body language that he wanted more than this. It was hard for her to be matter of fact. She managed.

'He was at the surgery when I got there.'

'Why? What was he doing there?'

'He's not well, I would imagine. Why else do people go to the doctor's?'

'Something serious, I hope,' said Frank.

'Frank,' said John, 'come on, enough, that's not nice.'

Frank conceded that this was true as he took the kebabs from Laura. She sighed, hoping she hadn't just caught his glance at John, sly and expectant, the start of a grin forming. She would have been disappointed at having done his work for him. John was his to play with. Nice one, Laura. The lamb hissed as it touched bars of the grill.

'He wouldn't apologise?' asked John.

'Refused, point blank,' she said.

'To a little girl?'

She shook her head.

The two brothers exchanged an almost identical shake of

the head, as though disbelief was a family trait.

'Can you believe that?' said John.

'I'd say you've got your work cut out there, little brother. Fuck. Neighbours like that.'

'Neighbour.'

Laura didn't say a word. She was waiting for the detonation and felt like she still had her finger on the button. She breathed slowly and shallowly to try to calm her heart, racing with her mind as she coped with escalating visions of how this could go.

'Maybe he's just been on his own too long.'

'What,' she said.

John's comment ran so contrary to what she had been expecting that it could only be called an implosion.

'Even if it's how he wants it,' said John, 'it's bound to affect him.'

'I, I suppose, no, I would say so, definitely,' she said, saying anything to agree with this new John who had suddenly appeared next to her. He actually sounded as though he was thinking about Luther. She could barely credit the words to his mouth. He stroked Molly's hair as he expanded on his theory.

'Probably has no idea how to talk to children.' John shifted in his seat so that he could see Laura and spoke to her instead of the world. 'Like the other night, you remember, the way he knelt down and talked to Molly, as though she understood?'

She nodded. He had been doing so well.

'I think he struggles with everybody,' she said.

'Except you.'

'John. Not again.'

'No, I'm being serious. You could be our way in. I don't

know what I could say.'

He snorted.

'What?'

'It's nothing. It's…' He stretched and grabbed with his fingers, trying to wrestle the words from the air between them. 'I'll bet this isn't what you expected our first few days to be like?'

'I didn't know what to expect,' she said, 'but no.'

She put her hand out. He took it and gave her a firm squeeze, which she returned.

'We'll just have to approach him in a different way,' he said. 'If you're not comfortable doing it on our behalf, well, we'll just leave the distance; let him come to us, if and when he's ready.'

More hissing as Frank turned the kebabs, apparently unaware of what John was saying. This thought was enough to make her doubt if she'd heard John correctly. Frank didn't miss anything. Yet there he was, on the verge of whistling by the purse of his lips, happily cooking their food. Had John excluded Frank on purpose? The possibility of him excluding Frank at all was dizzying and she suddenly felt suspicious. Were they working together? Had she been lulled into a trance? She still had hold of John's hand.

'You okay?' he said.

'Fine,' she said, wanting to believe she was. 'I think that's a good idea. Like you said, when he's ready.'

Frank came over with the platter of cooked kebabs. John took the one for Molly, snapping the point off the skewer before handing it to her in a doubled-over napkin. He handed one to Laura. Molly watched, then copied, holding her food sideways like a cob of corn, creating charred smears from ear to ear. The four of them ate in a silence that betrayed their hunger. She saw a butterfly; a ghostly flutter of white with sooty wing-tips. Swallows swept low in flight over the lochan chasing the same insects that caused the fish to break the surface, concentric circles spreading in the aftermath of their snatch. A tiny brown bird sang in the reeds and a handful of chaffinch came close in search of crumbs. John refilled their glasses. Maybe John had spoken to Frank. He wasn't himself, doing small talk as he passed around the remaining kebabs, collecting the used skewers. He wasn't looking for confrontation. After they had finished, Frank took their greasy napkins and threw them, along with the skewers, onto the still-hot coals. His attention on Molly, he laughed when she jumped as the crumpled white balls caught and burst into flames that rose and licked the inside of the barbeque hood, old fat spitting and popping. Her eyes danced orange.

An hour later she was asleep.

When Laura had filled the dishwasher, she went outside, drained her glass but declined another. She kissed John and waved over the table to Frank, who was pouring, thanking them both for a lovely night.

'It's been a long day,' she said. 'See you in the morning.'

She was yawning as she closed the sliding door, thinking what a strange evening it had been.

The strangeness seeped into her sleep, where Laura found herself voiceless and alone, pinned to the floor, face down, in a huge vault-like space of echoes of scuffles that bounced from unseen walls. Her hair was gripped in rough hands that pulled back, compressing her neck, exposing her throat, forcing her head to be still as she struggled to breathe beneath the crouching weight of the body on top of her, buckling her ribcage as it leant to be close to her ear. Gloved hands stroked her face with a false tenderness. It was laughing as her tears soaked into the leather; talking to her from this position of enforced intimacy, its words unclear, trapped in muffled bubbles like a malevolence undeciphered as it rammed its fingers into her mouth, preventing her cries. The weight shifted. Its grip loosened in response to a shuffling out of her sight, dragged footsteps across a rough floor; somebody else was watching. She was released as the burden turned liquid and poured from her. She sat up, blind and unsure, knowing the threat was gone yet unable to see or trust that which may be her protection. She was wrapped in warmth, able to breathe. There was absolute silence.

It was their quiet that woke her. John wasn't in bed. Frank's room was empty. Downstairs, the lights were still on. Their half-full glasses were still on the table. The house was deserted. A lumpen dread formed in her stomach.

Laura swung the front door open expecting to hear threats and arguments: the sounds of one man being goaded and abused by two drunks. Not the thin, dry crackle of timber burning.

Luther at the end of the boardwalk, floating, one ghost or another, above himself as he stared into the dark water; glass flat, rolling with clouds, slicked with patches of sun. Fish wound through the stanchions, in and out of shadow, over the spectral bow of the boat as it reached into the murk. It dissolved as the clinkered carcass sloped away with the steep bank of the lochan; the pale edge of the front thwart barely discernible, the two shotgun holes in the hull submerged.

The rotten end of a mooring rope swayed in the breeze, its raggy fibres barely disturbing the surface tension, as light as a pond skater.

Somewhere down there remained a red Wellington boot, once weighted with water, now mud-full and part of the floor, released from dungarees as he had pulled Ishbel out, too late. A mark showed over her eye, where she had banged her head, falling, trying to get into the boat on her own, trying to please daddy, to be grown up. Tarragh had called him back to clean up his mess. 'It'll wait,' he'd shouted, eager for them to be out in the boat, only to be told that it wouldn't, that she didn't like coming back into an untidy house, which he knew, and she was fed up telling him. He went back, leaving his camera on the boardwalk, telling Ishbel not to touch, not to move, to wait. He was too long and too late. Hunched over her as she lay across the wooden slats, cold and limp, his tears fused with his wet daughter, shaking as he tried to resuscitate her, already grieving. He had raised himself to kneeling at the sound of Tarragh running towards them.

'Look what you've done.'

It was the first blame, hurled like a stone.

She had called him away. But he had left her alone.

Luther wiped his eyes.

He was exhausted. Sleep no longer provided rest. The need to piss two or three times nightly was what usually saved him from the dreams. Tonight though, it wasn't his bladder. He had been wakened by their clumsy tiptoeing past his house. He was alert to their footsteps going silent and he surmised they had left the road and were about to attack. He waited for the creaking of the steps, the turning of his handle and the spread of moonlight across the floor that would mean they had come through the door. It didn't happen. He lay there for minutes. By the time Luther got out of bed and walked through the house without turning any lights on he could smell smoke. At the back window he rested his hands on the window-sill as he looked out. The four hives closest to the house were on fire. At the gate, darker than the night, a penumbra of fire-glow across their faces, John and Frank stood transfixed by the results of their handiwork. Sparks spat in every direction like burning bees too late in their escape. The rows receded away from the house like headstones, less distinct the further from the flames they were. John turned to the window. Luther could make out an ear, a cheek and a temple. Fire danced in the recess of John's eye socket. A moment passed. He reached over and tapped Frank. They turned and left. Luther followed their progress until they dropped down the driveway to the fully illuminated house. Laura sat on the porch step, her head in her hands. As they approached she stood to meet them. Whatever she said was roughly ignored as the two men barged past her on the way to the kitchen. She tried again as they reappeared with a beer each. She was dismissed with a wave of a hand, a few shouted words of rejection as they slumped onto the sunroom sofas.

When she appeared at the top of the staircase, Laura was wiping her eyes. He was glad she was crying. It told him she had nothing to do with it. Her forehead against the window, she looked outwards, trapped behind glass in artificial light. She waved. It was the second time Luther had seen her wave to him. It was as though she was saying goodbye. He leant across and put the kitchen light on. He waved back, glad to see her raise her head and manage a small wave in reply before disappearing into the bedroom corridor.

Luther poured a whisky, turned the light off and headed for the back door. Outside he sat on the step to watch the final stages of the cremation. The initial fury had died down. The smell was sweet. The heat was pleasant. There was no breeze at all. He sat through the sunrise. By which time the hives had disintegrated and all that remained were bull's eyes and charcoal embers, suspended from the sky by the final slender tendrils of smoke. As he stood over them Luther realised there had been no dawn chorus, as if the birds had sensed it would be inappropriate. Empty of bees, the morning was still and quiet. The day was waiting for a decision, an indication of how it should behave. Luther looked around and found he didn't care. He went inside.

When Laura came to the door he was sitting at the table. He had brewed coffee, poured whisky but drunk neither. His journal was open. He had written the date in the top right hand corner. Laura knocked three times. He put his pen down but stayed seated, not knowing what to say.

He was reminded of the days and weeks following Ishbel's burial. The people of the town came to the house with food, comfort and sympathy. Milton was a small community that had been shocked by the accident and it had acted accordingly. Some came once, others persisted. Clergy of all persuasions had put aside the fact that they neither attended church nor followed a creed and tried to be there for them, offered to pray for them. Their door was never locked, yet no one ever came in, grief being something you have to be invited to share. He and Tarragh sat at the table, ignoring the outside world, unable to speak to each other. They must have eaten. The visits stopped in the third week, the day Luther tried to kill a nun.

'Maybe this is a way of letting God into your life,' was all she said.

Her words still hung in the air as Luther almost wrenched the door from its hinges in his anger and pounced upon her. Luther had grabbed her by the throat with such force that they both fell to the floor. He had her pinned to the ground, crushing her windpipe as he spat the words at her bulging eyes.

'Fuck your God. I want nothing to do with him.'

Sister Mary Winifred was sixty-four. She fainted. Whether it was fear, shock or lack of oxygen, it saved her life. Limp in his hand so soon after he had held Ishbel's body, he'd fallen back, revolted, wiping his palm in the dirt. He scrambled to his feet. When the door slammed, the nun still lay on the floor, mouth open, her wimple coming loose from her grey hair.

'Do you think she wanted to help?' Tarragh had asked.

He hadn't answered. Luther had retreated to the cave and screamed until his throat bled. Even now, he still had no idea how long she lay there. He wasn't in jail, so she didn't die. It was after the nun that Tarragh started to drink with a purpose. A brief period of acclimatisation led into days of numbness connected by frayed threads of sleep.

Laura knocked again.

'Luther? Are you there? Luther, I'm sorry. I hope you can hear me. I had no idea what they were going to do. You know that. They kept it to themselves until I'd gone to bed. I should have seen something was wrong, Frank being so pleasant. I know it was his idea. Though that doesn't excuse John, he's old enough to know better. Listen to me, trying to make things better.'

Luther picked his pen up and wrote the first words of the day. '*It wasn't your fault.*'

'How did we fuck this up so quickly?'

She waited for Luther to answer.

He looked to the base of the door where her feet disturbed the light coming underneath. She moved away and he thought she had gone. When Laura's face appeared in the kitchen window, he was surprised, and he couldn't hold her gaze. His eyes fixed on what he had written. He listened to her as she moved around the house, pushing through the bushes and shrubs that grew close to the walls. When the sounds of movement stopped, he knew she was at the front window, her face level with his, waiting.

'I'm sorry,' she said. 'I can't help that you find it hard to look at me.'

'I don't.'

He placed his pen in the centre ridge of the journal and pushed the chair back from the table.

Luther pulled the sash window up as high as it would go. Kneeling in front of Laura, he traced the contours of her face with his hand, moving down over her lips, the line of her neck, ending on the small scar.

'I could look at you all day.'

She tried to smile.

'I'm glad.'

'There's no need for the guilt or the sadness,' he said, 'It wasn't you.'

'I know.' She sighed heavily and he thought she was going to break down. 'I knew that last night. Thank you, for waving.'

'I waved back.'

Laura glanced to her right, making sure she couldn't be seen. She gripped the sill, pulling herself close to stand right against the house, inches from Luther. He could feel her breath, the strength of her voice when a whisper would have been enough.

'Could you kiss me?' she said. 'Would that be okay?'

'I'd like that.'

'I mean me.'

'So do I.'

Luther kissed Laura on the lips. It was a kiss between two people who didn't know what was going to happen next.

'Thank you,' she said, 'that makes me feel better.'

Laura stood back.

'I should go.'

As she stepped out of the shrubbery and long grass onto his path she looked back. Dew stained her shorts and shone on her legs.

'What are you going to do?' she asked.

'I don't know.'

'But something?'

He nodded.

'I won't hurt you,' he said. 'I won't hurt Molly.'

'I don't want you to be hurt.'

'Too late for that.'

He stood as soon as she turned away. He tried not to rush to the window over the sink but he didn't want to let her go. He didn't want her to go back to him, standing on his porch in his dressing gown, arms akimbo. John was already talking at her and gesticulating at Luther's house before she was half way down the drive. She retaliated with a dismissive wave of her arm and looked to Luther to be more than holding her own in the argument until he hit her with a slap so severe that it nearly took her off her feet.

Frank whooped from where he'd been sitting in the sunroom.

Molly had seen it and knew how Laura felt. She was crying on the other side of the porch, her fingers streaking the glass. John was genuinely surprised by his attack, confused, holding his hand away from himself, disgusted, as if it had suddenly developed a mind of its own. He came off the step to try and hold her. Laura avoided his arms, beating them away. Her eyes watered. Her face stung.

'Get away from me.'

She glared at him, her heart pounding. Her fist clenched instinctively, ready to fight.

'Laura, I'm so sorry, I...'

'John,' said Frank as he came through the doorway and pushed his way past his brother, 'what's the point of hitting her if you're going to say you're sorry? It's as if you didn't mean it.' Frank continued across the grass, onto the bridge, along the boardwalk, whistling. John wilted. He looked like shit. Keeping up with Frank was taking its toll.

'I didn't. Laura you have to believe me, I don't know where that came from. I'm hung-over, not enough sleep. That wasn't me, you know that. I've never hit you.'

'That was you,' she said. 'Maybe you think he's right; I deserve it, for something.'

'No.'

'NO.'

Laura spun around at the sound of Luther's raised voice. He was in the lane, pointing at Frank at the end of the boardwalk where he was unbuttoning his jeans.

'STOP. I'll not have that – stop now. I said stop now.'

Frank gave Luther the finger, let his jeans drop around his ankles and proceeded to relieve himself into the lochan. Luther ran into his house, reappearing seconds later with his shotgun, which was already up at his shoulder and the trigger pulled before any of them knew what was happening. Laura jumped at the explosion. Frank screamed and collapsed through the arc of his own piss as lead shot tore into the planking and his right boot. He got halfway to his feet and was running as best he could towards the house, dragging his leg with one hand, holding his jeans up with his other when a second deafening shot splintered through the boardwalk just behind him. He fell hard. Laura saw Luther reloading the shotgun. She ran. She ran to where Frank was struggling to get back up, calling at Luther to stop, not to shoot anymore. In a matter of seconds she stood breathless between him and Frank, her hands up, begging him not to shoot again, knowing she was in his sight as he raised the barrels for another shot. John arrived, dressing gown flapping, berating her for being so stupid, shocked when she elbowed him back behind her, using herself as a shield. He helped Frank to his feet, taking his weight, leading him back to the house. Luther lifted his head. He was too far away for her to be sure but she thought he was shaking. He lowered the gun, broke the barrel from the stock and allowed it to swing to his side.

Laura found Molly, head bowed, sitting on the floor behind the sofa and the stone wall of the old Macpherson place. No longer crying, she was repeatedly pushing her fingers into the plush pile of the carpet. When Laura asked if she wanted to come and sit with mummy, she put her arms up for Laura to lift her, whereas an hour before she would have toddled around. Molly flinched at the noise coming from the kitchen as Laura picked her up. She kicked the door closed against Frank's cursing and swearing, guessing that John was pulling his boot off. He had been lucky. Only a few pellets of shot looked to have broken the leather. The boot may have saved his foot. He didn't sound like he felt lucky.

Sinking into the sofa, Laura settled Molly onto her lap and held her close, trying to stop the trembling. They sat for a few minutes as the ruckus peaked and then began to die down, their voices dwindling to a murmur as they inspected the wound.

John called her name as he did a circuit of the house looking for her. She didn't answer, knowing he would find her before long. When he realised where she was, he opened the door and popped his head in, as though he didn't want to intrude. He struggled to look her in the eye.

'Hey,' he said.

'Hey.'

'I'm going to take Frank to the doctor's.'

She nodded. He gestured to Molly.

'She okay?'

'Not really.'

'Can I come in?'

'It's our house, John. You don't need to ask.'

He sat near her, leaning forward with his elbows on his knees, staring at the floor between his feet. He rubbed his hands together, dry palms sliding across each other, anxious and sibilant. Twice, he went to say something but couldn't. It got stuck in his throat. She sensed him turn his head halfway around, looking up at her. Staring at some point in space in front of her, she knew he could see his hand-print still red across her face.

'It won't matter how many times I say I'm sorry, will it?' he said.

'Does it make any difference how many times I do?'

He slumped back, his head on the sofa and sighed.

'Why do you think it always boils down to that?'

'Doesn't it?'

'No,' he said.

Frank called from the front door, 'John, you ready?'

'Be right there. You get in the car.' He sat forward and met Laura's gaze. 'Honestly. It doesn't.'

She didn't know if she believed him.

'Are you going to go to the police?'

'Don't know,' he said. 'You think I should?'

She shrugged.

'You think it would help more if I didn't?'

'Depends what you want,' she said. 'You wouldn't have to admit to arson.'

'I suppose.' John leant across and kissed Molly before he got up. She thought he was going to leave it at that but he turned back at the doorway. 'Even you have to admit though; it's a bit extreme, shooting somebody for taking a piss.'

Laura shook her head.

'It wasn't about that.'

'What? You think it was his beehives still?'

'No. There's a bigger picture.'

'Go on, enlighten me.'

'The lochan. The end of the boardwalk, where Frank was pissing, his trousers around his ankles, not thinking about anything or anyone but himself.'

'I know, that was out of order, I'll talk to him about it.'

'It's where Luther's daughter drowned – her name was Ishbel, she was four years old.'

For a moment he didn't believe her, she could tell. Why would he want to? He blinked, glanced from her to Molly, closed his eyes and fell against the doorjamb, head back, throat exposed. He flinched when Frank pressed the horn, three long blasts.

'All right,' he shouted. He groaned as he saw Molly tense and pull herself tighter into Laura, who had a look of consternation.

'Jesus, John. Could you make her any more scared?'

'I know, I know, I'm sorry.'

He closed his eyes and took a deep breath in a conscious effort to calm himself. He put his arms out to Molly, slowly, not wanting to surprise or scare her any further.

'Daddy get a hug?'

Molly shook her head and hid her face. Laura didn't offer him any comfort. *I don't blame you, darling*, she thought, combing her fingers through the wispy blond curls of Molly's hair. *I really don't.*

John stared at them, his arms falling back to his sides.

'How did you know he wouldn't shoot you?'

'I didn't,' said Laura. 'I just knew he wouldn't want to.'

'I don't understand.'

Frank sounded the horn again. John clenched his teeth at his brother's impatience but she was relieved.

'You should go,' she said.

Luther spied the white handkerchief sticking out of the

ground just beyond the mossy overhang of the left hand bank. He climbed down the side of the falls. With no obvious dry route across, he used stepping stones to get him part-way before dropping into the water mid-stream, to continue, shin-deep. He surmised the bank-side erosion had occurred during the last winter, January no doubt, when rain had fallen for most of the month and the swollen torrent would have reshaped the river.

The same undercutting had destabilised the root system of the rowan tree that had crashed across the stream. The stronger boughs, jammed in between rock folds and accumulated fluvial debris, held the trunk above the water while the slender upper branches bowed over the opposite bank like a weary head, the whole image reminiscent of a figure performing a press-up, or worshipping at an altar. Although the root fan, its toes deep in the stream, had been washed clean of soil, the tree still strived to live, fed by the thirsty filaments that moved in the current like clean hair.

Luther waded across to the base of the grey–brown trunk. Leaning on it as he bent to retrieve the handkerchief, he felt there was some give. He could rock it with ease. The tree was finely balanced and it was obvious to him that this coming winter, maybe sooner, the tree would be dislodged from the land completely. When it dropped it would form a triangular dam against the left bank, its sharp shape at odds with the swirls and curls of the stream it would divert. The level would rise against the bank, forcing the icy water to pour through the newly created skylight into the underground walkway and cave system. From the angle of this fresh crack in the ceiling of sedimentary rock and the amount of steps he knew it to be to the cavern he worked out where the cavern was. It was back across the stream, beneath a smooth apron of grass that was a popular summer campsite for those visitors who failed to take the midge into consideration before pitching their tent. A steel lorry wheel that lay on its side, lifted from the ground by three flat boulders, was used to contain the camp-fires. Half a dozen or so disposable barbeques were flattened and kept in place by another rounder and heavier boulder, the start of a tin foil cairn.

The stream concertinaed back into itself like a snake. Luther didn't blame it. Were he the stream, he would resist the journey downhill, hold on to this final stretch, carve troughs and basins in which to sink below the primary flow, delaying the inevitable. Luther knew what a poor reception the sad little town of Milton had in wait for its clear, sparkling beauty. The sole point of welcome and appreciation for its flow was when it made their ornamental mill wheel turn, over and over, changeless and pointless. Things changed. It was offensive to give potency or relevance to that which didn't; particularly something that no longer did the job it was fashioned for. Climbing from the water, he turned and relieved himself into the Piper's Pool.

Lying on this small patch of natural lawn, his head sank into that pillow of detached quiet just above ground level that suggests another world. The sweet and incongruous smell of coconut that fell from the gorse wafted across the glade. He remembered the smell bringing a giggle to their conversation. It didn't belong here. Coconuts in a glen, halfway up a wind-ravaged, sun-starved mountainside. Coconuts; it was wrong, but it was beautiful. Relaxation allowed the falls to tumble into his left ear and make his head swim before they gurgled out and away from his right. Luther wondered how many people had lain here, fishermen waiting, drunks snoring, families listening, couples conceiving; all oblivious of her lying below them, at peace. His eyes watered beneath the strength of the sun. The cloudless sky was sewn to the trees with the cross-stitch of bird's flight; finches, warblers and tits, courting and nesting in anticipation of young to feed, ever mindful of the slate blue dash of the sparrowhawk. Male grasshoppers sang of territory and desire in the late morning heat.

Luther absorbed the warmth of the day and felt the tension easing. His right hand uncurled enough for the gun to slip from his grip.

She was glad Frank had been kept in. An overnight stay in the cottage hospital was what they all needed. John had tried to laugh about him sharing the ward with the elderly permanent residents but Laura could see the strain on his face. He kept glancing at her cheek as if he'd see his hand-print; maybe it was still red. It no longer stung. The shouting, the slap, the gunshots, the screaming, Molly's fear; they all filled the house. Unable yet to find a way to talk to Laura, John sat at the computer researching how much it would cost to replace the hives, how practical it would be to source new bees. Molly climbed off the sofa and walked across to see the pictures of bees and hives and honey. She stood next to John, captivated by the screen. She leant an arm on his thigh and he put his hand around her shoulders, part-way forgiven.

They stayed like this for the best part of an hour, getting used to each other again. John typed with one hand, explained things to her, let her move and click with the mouse. Laura sat on the sofa. To her left her husband and daughter, to her right framed by the door to the snug, the boardwalk curved over the water in a tableau of sun, shadow and reflection.

Luther's head was bowed when he came into view, crossing their garden to gain access to the boardwalk before heading out, over their lochan. He didn't once look towards the house. When he stopped at the end and looked down, Laura knew exactly where Ishbel had died.

'John,' she said.

'Mmm.'

'Come here.'

From the noise he made, he practically jumped out of his chair, lifting Molly as he did, so eager was he to please her.

'Sure, what is it?'

He was about to sit next to Laura when she pointed outside.

'Look.'

John remained standing as he followed her lead.

Luther stood motionless in the afternoon sun. The breeze disturbed his hair, flattened his shirt against his chest and lifted his collar.

'Jesus, that's awful.'

'Poor man,' she said, 'he looks so small.'

'Lost.'

'It doesn't seem right,' she said, 'a day like today, such a lovely place and all he feels is pain. It makes the whole place sad, don't you think?'

'I know what you mean. Should I close the door?'

'Why?'

'Well,' he said, 'it's a private moment, don't you think?

'I don't think he cares anymore. Besides, it's more than a

moment.'

Laura stood as John leant back and rested on the arm of the sofa with Molly on his knee. She went and stood in the doorway and studied Luther, a fallen, wingless angel, communing with the past.

Trapped bubbles escaped as her body rolled in the water like felled lumber. Facing the sky, it was plain her face was injured. The smooth indent that sank into her forehead had barely bruised, meaning little time between the blow and death.

The event had been a rare and short-lived moment of fear. Moorhen had taken to the reeds, dragonflies vanished and the birds of the surrounding woodland fallen silent. By the time she was missed, the last of the ripples barely registered on the glassy surface as they soaked into the sand of the far bank.

Down below, as she cooled and paled, she looked to be at peace, her face dappled by the refracted sunlight, her eyelashes long and soft enough to drift with the current without raising their lids. Wavelets coursed through the wet red of her T-shirt, causing it to rise and fall in a tease of mock-breathing. The faint dimple at the corner of her mouth almost convinced him that she was playing a game, that waiting long enough would see it deepen, pulled by some internal thread into her infectious smile: followed by a laugh that was pearl bright, skylark happy and chest deep.

A second splash preceded the howling.

She was heaved from the shallows in a rush of sound. Her hair hung long and straight and her limbs flopped, still connected to the lochan that poured from her in silver ribbons, filled her lungs and spilled over baby teeth from the dark recess of her open mouth.

The arms that held her pulled her close to forever feel her weight.

Molly slipped from John's knee, crossing to put her hand into Laura's as the wind picked up, ribbing the lochan's surface, bobbing the moorhen back amongst the reeds. Cloud shadows took the edge off the glare and momentarily dulled the vibrancy of the land against the blue and white of the sky. When they'd blown over and the colours reasserted themselves, Luther appeared even darker, blackly defiant to the sun's effect.

'What happened to his wife?'

'She left,' said Laura, not taking her eyes off Luther. 'One day she just wasn't there anymore. Mr Cargill said his mind snapped. He was walking around the village at all times of the day and night, summer into winter, calling out her name, unravelling, knocking on doors, convinced somebody was hiding her. They took pity on him and began telling him that she would come back one day, when she was ready. He walked into the church one Sunday morning. He hadn't shaved or washed for weeks.'

'Jesus.'

'He said to them, 'You don't know where she is, do you?' Nobody did. He nodded, turned and left, out of the church, out of the village. Next thing they knew he'd bought all the land, stopped people using the road. He cut himself off, completely.'

John didn't say anything. The silence grew and she could feel him looking at her.

'What?'

'I was just wondering if there was anything you didn't

know.'

'You and Frank were sleeping,' she said, 'and Mr Cargill was happy to talk.' Laura glanced away from Luther and pointed at her handbag on the coffee table. 'You pass me my bag please?'

John leant over and dragged the bag by its strap until it fell from the table and swung it into his grip as he stood. He walked over to Laura and handed it to her. She unzipped it and took a photo from an inside pocket, which she handed to John. Molly went to his side, using his trouser leg to pull herself onto tiptoes, craning to see the picture. John held it lower so she could see, looking from the image to Laura and back again.

'That's her,' John said, 'isn't it?'

'And Luther and…'

'Cargill, I know. I'd recognise him anywhere.'

He let Molly hold the photograph. She held it up to Laura, grinning.

'Beeman.'

'Yes, beeman,' said Laura. 'Bzzz, bzzz.'

'Bzzz. Bzzz.'

Molly put the picture on the table and knelt down to examine it.

'That's uncanny,' said John. 'That's what you meant, why he wouldn't shoot you?'

'Why I didn't think he would.'

The sound of a car approaching caused Laura's shoulders to tighten. *Please let it not be Frank*. It continued past their house and she relaxed. The car's arrival broke the spell Luther had been under. It looked to Laura as though he said something to the water before he left. Maybe he spoke to her a lot. Today didn't have to be the first time. John had been right though. She wished she hadn't seen it.

Luther pushed the open door wide open, inviting Dr Shah to step inside. He didn't close it as he followed the doctor in. The doctor took a seat at the table. Luther closed the journal, made coffee, placed the doctor's in front of him and sat so they faced each other. Dr Shah gestured his thanks and took a sip. He placed his cup in front of him before he spoke.

'What is it you are you playing at, Mr Grove?'

'I don't follow, Dr Shah.'

'Hah. You don't follow.' He leant forward, his hands on the table. 'You think because you are not well you can take pot shots to kill others? Do you?'

Luther swallowed hot coffee and put his cup down.

'I wasn't trying to kill him, Ali, you know that. I was getting him away from her.'

Ali sat back and sighed.

'Well, lucky for you he is going to be fine. I got all the pellets that broke his skin.'

'I didn't ask. I don't care.'

Reaching down to the floor at his side, Luther produced a bottle of whisky and gestured to Ali. He declined, smiling. He took another sip as Luther poured whisky into his own coffee.

'Will you ever stop this trying to get me to join you in this bad habit?'

'It's just a habit,' said Luther. 'You need to learn to enjoy them.'

'Oh,' said Ali, observing Luther over the top of his glasses, 'and what are we now, a motivational speaker? Living life the Luther way, is it?'

Ali's suggestion tickled Luther. He soon shook with laughter, spilling coffee on his leg, which burned. The pain of this only served to make him laugh even more, to the degree that he had to put his cup down, even though he was unable to let go, he was shaking so much. Ali's laughter was reduced to a smile long before Luther had peaked and he had to wait, sipping his drink, for the fit to be spent. Eventually they faced each other across the table.

'That felt good, I would say?'

'Aye,' said Luther, wiping his eyes with his free hand, 'it did.'

'You should try it more often.'

'One joke doesn't make life a comedy, Ali. Nice try though.'

The silence that settled between them gave each the time to return to the truth of the situation. Ali spoke first.

'Tell me, has it got to the stage where it is hurting all the time?'

Luther didn't answer. His eyes prickled. He felt like everything about him hurt. It was how he knew he was still there.

'I am meaning the new pain,' said Ali.

'It's getting that way.'

'And you are still determined not to undertake the treatment?'

'Yes. More so.'

'How, more so?'

'I'm finding it harder.' Luther gestured toward the new house, it being explanation enough. 'You've seen her. She was at your surgery.'

'Yes. She is very striking.'

'They both are.'

'Doesn't that make it easier?'

'No,' said Luther, with a slow shake of his head.

Ali pushed the journal aside. He took a paper bag from his jacket pocket and shook two boxes onto the tabletop.

'A month's worth. Come to me if you need more.'

'Are they strong?'

'They should help,' said Ali. 'Please. Do not take more than the recommended daily allowance.'

Both men stared at the boxes rather than each other. Both men drained their cups.

'More coffee?'

'No, enough for me. Thank you.' Ali leant across and put his hand over Luther's. Luther could feel the slightest tremble in the smooth skin of Ali's warm hands. 'I would like to see you again, Mr Grove. No appointment needed.'

'You look tired,' said Luther, placing his other hand over that of the doctor. 'This your last call?'

'My last call today, yes. And last call of the week.' Ali pushed his chair back and stood. 'Thank you for the coffee.'

'You're welcome. Here.' Luther went to the kitchen and lifted a box, presenting it to Ali. It contained Kilner jars of preserved fruit and vegetables, individually wrapped in newspaper to stop them cracking against each other.

'I was going to bring it around. You've saved me the journey.' Ali's arms hung down by his sides. 'Please. It's good fruit. It would be a shame to waste it.'

As Ali brought his forearms up beneath the box and gripped the front, Luther was reminded of the weight in his own hands as he had carried Ishbel, the fire in his biceps that became his focus as he had walked from the church to the graveyard, refusing to allow Tarragh to touch the coffin. They thought he was taking the burden, protecting her.

'There's something else,' said Luther, indicating towards the journal. 'It's nearly finished. If you could read it I'd be grateful. Someone should know.'

Ali swallowed.

'Are you doing a good thing, Luther Grove?'

Behind the spectacles, through growing tears, Luther could see real doubt and knew the doctor was speaking as a friend. This hurt him, offended him.

'It's the right thing, Ali.'

There was no attempt to change his mind, which would have been futile. Ali, lips closed and breath held, raised his eyebrows before exhaling. The two men stared at each other, sharing half a grin. He hugged the jars of fruit to himself, nodded to Luther.

Luther watched Ali walk down the path to his car. He placed the box on the passenger seat and semi-secured it with the seat belt. The car moved away. He heard it manoeuvre in the rear gateway; Ali grinding the gears as usual as he reversed back out, before it reappeared, passing across the bright doorframe. When he was gone, Luther washed the cups and left them upturned on the draining board. This done, he sat at the table and opened the journal. He wrote the date.

There are a few final things that need to be said. Firstly, I would like to apologise to Doctor Ali Shah, a good man, both as doctor and friend, for the theft of painkillers from his surgery; a deceitful and ignoble act against a man who has always been fair and straight with me.

Four hours later Luther's head was almost empty. It was late evening. His hair was stuck to his scalp and his T-shirt soaked up dust.

He went down into the cellar and came back with a potato box, partially filled with the remaining jars of preserved fruit. Each jar had a white label on the lid with 'Laura' written in black block capitals. He bound the journal in brown paper and wrote 'ALI SHAH' across the front before he placed it in the box. Going to the kitchen he pulled a handful of manila envelopes and document folders from the bottom drawer in the kitchen, his filing cabinet. He didn't close it. It hung open like a ransacked vault.

Back at the table, he used the paperwork to pack everything so nothing could shatter. He gripped the sides of the box, ready to lift it, but couldn't move. He knew that as long as he left the drawer open the strength to lift wouldn't be there. He let go and hid his face behind his hands, closing his eyes against the bars of blood-filtered sunshine, rubbing them deep into their sockets until it hurt. When he stopped, retinal fireworks, negative images and distorted humour, burned out, developed and righted themselves until his vision was as clear as if it had been washed.

A roll's worth of sellotape, stretched and twisted into a taut wrapping, had dried around the photograph album. Transparent flakes birled in the draught like fish scales as he lifted it from the drawer, the house's only treasure. The remaining bands of dried adhesive shone. He pushed his thumbnail against the tape and it cracked like mica.

Tarragh, perched above him on a rock at the peak of Creagh Dhubh, seemingly standing in the sky, arms outstretched, face shrouded in hair, the clouds racing over her giving the impression she was about to fly or fall. He recalled how light-headed he felt taking that photograph: and the sickly sweet breath of the white horse as it strained over the fence to take grass from Ishbel's hand, cupped inside his; the series of pictures Tarragh captured when the horse pulled back sharply as the barbed wire pierced its neck, causing Ishbel to fall backwards and roll down through the long grass of the embankment, dizzy but giggling when she came to rest; the final close up of the crimson stain; Tarragh lying on her rug, sunk amongst buttercups, her head hidden in the meadow outside Milton, the swell of her pregnancy higher in the frame than the three creags across the valley; Ishbel sitting on a stack of drying peat blocks in the South Uist sun, leaning forward to see down into the fresh black scar that cut across the boggy moorland, knowing he was in there, waiting to jump up and surprise her. They played the game for almost an hour, her hysteria escalating until the inevitable fall. He climbed out of the hole exhausted and filthy, his feet soaked, his trousers stained fast. That peat was still beneath his nails. Tarragh singing Johnny Cash as she drove, the road ahead reflected in her sunglasses; Tarragh on a picnic, both cheeks stuffed with his cheese roll that she had tried to finish before he got back from having a pee out of sight, in deference to the other picnickers. He had retaliated by drinking all the juice, making her eat her way through the doughy mouthful as punishment; Ishbel, his arm around her waist, standing on the red plastic chairs of the Eriskay ferry, peering over the enamelled safety rails, fascinated by the churning foam of the water; a frame of green, looking down the grassy hillside of Creag Mhor, with Milton in the distance; Tarragh striding up towards him in her shorts, boots and bra, T-shirt tucked into her belt; Tarragh, a couple of yards further up, laughing, white teeth beneath the blur of her bra as she whirled it above her head.

He didn't need to open it. He tilted it in the light. The desiccated tape caught the day like weathered lacquer.

Wrapped in brown paper, he wrote 'Laura' on it and placed it in the box alongside the journal. He had no idea what she would make of it, or do with it. As far as he was concerned, it was the truth. He wanted her to see who he had been. It would make more sense to her if Ali followed Luther's wishes. Ali would get Luther's journal, a version of what had happened after; the explanation he felt he owed him. A single event separated both books. Together they could complete a story.

Main Street was quiet. The surgery was locked but not alarmed. Sliding his knife between the sash windows, Luther had no trouble getting in. He left the box on Ali Shah's desk. It would be Monday until he became a doctor again, possibly sooner, though Luther doubted it. However, just in case, Luther lifted the box from the desk and put it onto the examination table, pulling the curtain across to hide it. Looking at it, he knew the blue curtain would be the first thing the doctor would see when he came in. He gathered it back along its rail until only the headrest was hidden and dragged the box behind it. He couldn't find it straightaway. What Luther was about to do was already written. If Ali Shah read it, he would have to try and stop him.

Laura was biting her nails, something she hadn't done for over a year. They'd eaten, the kitchen had been cleared and the heat was leaving the day, yet she wasn't sure what she'd done all afternoon. She still felt dazed, slightly removed.

At least John had finally stopped talking. Since the doctor had pulled away from Luther's house all she had heard was his pocket education on beekeeping, conducted over the phone with the handful of suppliers he had canvassed regarding the replacement and restocking of the hives he had destroyed. Her only moment of respite was when John actually admitted to somebody what had happened, what he had done. The resulting lecture had shamed John into mumbling one or two-syllable words of apology and shame. The man refused to sell John hives or bees. Whoever it was, Laura wanted his number.

He came through to her, happy with the way his afternoon had gone, convinced that the couple of hours' work was effort enough to expunge his actions of the previous night.

'I think it's sorted. They'll ring to confirm a delivery date tomorrow, but with a bit of luck they should be here midweek.'

'That's…' was all she managed before she shuddered, her arms and shoulders twisting through the air in a momentary loss of control.

'Someone walk over your grave?'

'No, just don't feel quite right.'

'Might be shock.'

'I don't think so,' she said, rubbing her arms.

'You want a fleece?'

'Mmm, that would be good – there's one in the kitchen.'

How could she tell him she was scared when she didn't

know what she was scared of? She didn't feel brave or sure anymore.

John came back and draped the fleece over her shoulders

'Thanks.'

'He's back, by the way.'

'Sorry?'

'Luther, he's back. I saw you looking.'

A couple of hours ago, Luther had left. She'd heard his Defender turning over and pulling away. There was something about the sound, impatience or anger even, in the way he fired the engine. She'd gone to the door and looked up at Luther's home. Although he was gone he'd left his front door wide open. The place looked abandoned.

The scream of the chainsaw cut through them. Laura was on her feet, running back out to the porch, almost falling as her socks slipped on the floor. John followed. He stood behind her. Luther was slicing through the seasoned timber that had been the first point of altercation, only two days ago, with a singular determination. Logs fell to the floor, followed a second later by a dull thud as he worked his way through the wood without pausing or raising his head from his work.

'Do you think everything's all right?' said Laura.

'Best to do it while it's dry, I suppose.'

She didn't answer.

'That's not what you mean, is it?'

'No,' she said. 'He's different.' She wanted to ask John if he thought Luther could have shot her, because now she wasn't sure. She swallowed and willed the tears to stop, steadied the quiver in her chin. She pulled the fleece tight around her and used the excuse of still feeling the cold to turn away and go back into the snug. As she stepped onto the carpet Molly peeked up at her and grinned.

When the screaming stopped the stillness of the afternoon was punctuated by the rhythmic chop of the axe as the wood was split. When the chopping stopped, John slid the glass wall of the sunroom open. He stuck his head into the room where she had been trying to doze and persuaded her to come and sit outside with him.

He'd prepared a cold platter: smoked salmon, olives, crusty bread, gherkins and some sliced salad.

'Looks nice, she said, 'thank you.'

'Thank you,' he said, handing her a glass of champagne, 'for saving Frank's life.'

'Jesus, was that today? Feels like so long ago.'

'I know,' he said, leaning to kiss her, 'and you'll probably regret it.'

'More than once.'

John agreed.

The heat in the sinking sun relaxed her nape and shoulders. A woodpecker chiselled a rat-tat-tat through the bark of a nearby tree. Damselfly skimmed the surface of the lochan, bouncing angular, mid-air as though in some invisible pinball machine; trout surfaced to snatch the gnats that paddled in the still of the evening. Molly managed to guide a whole spoonful of chopped boiled egg into her mouth. John was quiet. It was turning into the kind of evening she had hoped to have, before they had moved. She heard distant, deliberate footsteps. Over her shoulder, Laura noticed that Luther's door was still open, showing the inner dark. He stepped out with the regular coils of a rope slung over his shoulder. He walked around the side of his house, across the unused foundations and through the gap in the dry stone wall. He climbed the hillside, parallel to the treeline, before he dipped left into the cover of the woods.

Luther dropped the coiled rope on the bank and slid the machete from its sheath. Working quickly, he felled and finished a sapling until he had a straight pole the same height as himself, the width of his arm. Jamming it into a rabbit hole he tried it for flexibility and was satisfied there was little give.

He stood behind the fallen rowan that was balanced above and downstream of the crack that allowed light into his tunnel. He guided the bough into the space beneath the tree at about forty-five degrees, adjusting its position until it slipped into a natural groove in the rock that would act as a fulcrum. Tying a rolling hitch around the top of the new lever, he threw the rope over a thick overhanging bough about ten feet away. The coils unravelled against the clear sky. As it fell to the ground, the weight of the rope was enough to hold the bough in position. Luther stepped out of the water.

With the line pulled taut, he threaded the free end through the crack into the passageway to the cave until there was no slack, using one of the removed branches to secure it. Luther washed his hands and cupped a couple of mouthfuls to drink. He ran wet fingers through his hair. When the tree fell it would make a significant difference to the flow. He smirked, almost wishing he could be there when their wheel stopped turning.

They were still sitting outside when he strode down the hill. From the corner of his eye he could see she was looking at him. He went straight into the house.

Within a couple of hours, Luther had finished hauling the day's chopped logs through the passageway to the cave. He dragged a final four-foot stump with the aid of an old steel towing cable from an even older Defender. It was heavy and each bounce, over the smallest of ridges, caused him to pause, wincing as the cable dug into his shoulder and the cut to his thumb reopened again. Wringing with sweat, he dropped it as soon as he entered the cave and slumped to the floor, feeling weak and tired. He took some of Ali's tablets, which he had emptied loose into his pocket. When he was able, using the light from the Tilley lamps, he built a fire in the pit, one that would roar, keep them both warm. He worked in silence, uttering not a word to Tarragh.

Leaving one lamp behind, Luther took the others and left.

Upstairs, he made the bed, swept the floor, wiped every surface and closed all doors and drawers.

Showered, shaved and dressed in fresh clothes, Luther sat at his table staring out of the door, eating plain oatcakes and sipping whisky, waiting for it to get dark.

She'd seen Luther swaying from the end of his rope, death-stained and dappled, moved by the breeze or the residual momentum of his final kicks. Would he kick? Would he grip the noose as it tightened and broke his Adam's apple? Could he embrace the end?

Hesitant steps in the church-like silence, hooves brushing through dried pine needles. Deer sniffing, before licking his toes as finches and tits appeared from nowhere to perch on him, pecking at shirt buttons, pulling at the stray hair strands that had fallen across his forehead, shitting down his arm or across his chest, until such time as everything was swept away by the satin, glove-like primaries of the gathering corvidae; corbies in search of eyes. With not enough to go around, his body would become an aerial battleground.

Her head had spun and her breath caught when he'd burst through the tree-line and stomped his way back down to his house, very much the living Luther, no longer carrying the rope. The fear of finding him had vanished. But he still swung in her mind, from shadow to shadow, breaking thin shafts of light. The patio heating was on, Molly slept and the glass wall was closed against the insects of the night, yet he was all she could see. She tried to distract herself with a magazine as she picked at the remains of the food.

The sweet smell of burning wood seeped in even though the house was sealed. They both smelled it at the same time, catching each other's eyes over the breakfast counter. Laura glanced down the kitchen to the sunroom and saw wisps of smoke drifting by, spiralling across the glass like cigarette smoke traversing a saloon ceiling.

Every remaining beehive was ablaze. The night air was still. From the porch, they could see vertical columns of dirty orange smoke racing up to the heavens where it cooled and spread, falling back to earth like hell-born snow.

They ran up the drive to the wall of his garden. Each hive was burning like a refinery outlet, forming rows of warning beacons. The roar of the flames was punctuated by the outward spit of crackling sparks firing through the demented spiralling of the final homeless bees. The grass steamed.

'Go and see if he's between the hives somewhere,' said Laura.

'Why?'

'John, he might need help.'

'I should care?'

'Just do it.'

She pushed past him, through the gate and into Luther's house.

She switched the lights on. The emptiness of the rooms stopped her dead. He was gone. She shivered and sweat ran cold down her back. She turned the lights off. Outside John was running the length of the wall, looking into the garden, coughing and shielding his eyes from the heat as he squinted between the hives. She crouched down and crawled along, looking up the length of the garden in case Luther had fallen behind a hive, out of sight. It was clear. Nothing interrupted the brassy glow of the grass. She stood up and saw that John had got to the end. When he turned to where she stood and held his hands out, shaking his head to indicate there was no sign of Luther, John looked trapped. Laura waved him back before he was condemned to an existence within the flames. Ducking and using his arms to shield his face he managed to get back to her. As they met at the gate the sound of the two-tones came around the mountain from the direction of Milton. Blue lights flashed between the trunks of the roadside trees. A line of cars had parked on the roadside. Exhaust fumes puffed in headlights. Drivers and passengers stood watching.

Twenty-two tons of barely used, highly polished fire appliance turned off the main road and ground through the path, creating its own ruts. It stopped just beyond their gate. The diesel engine growled. Beneath the blue lights, the doors opened as the air brakes hissed. Picked out by the full beams that pinned them to Luther's as though they were trying to escape from the scene of a crime, Laura felt guilty. Fire-fighters jumped out of the back cab like giddy storm troopers, flushed with the chance to tackle a real blaze, shouting textbook instructions as they guided the driver. An officer climbed out of the front. As soon as his door had closed the driver reversed down their drive, getting as close as he could to the lochan without leaving the hard standing. The brakes hissed again and the engine register changed, making the appliance sound more like an idling boat. The crew proceeded to run a line of hose from the appliance up to Luther's; the driver screwed a strainer onto a rigid suction tube and dropped its end into the water, the splash followed by a stream of rising bubbles.

The officer walked towards them, an ominous silhouette against the skyward lights of the appliance. The closer he got to them and the burning hives the more they could make him out. Cargill wasn't smiling at Laura. His eyes fixed on the hives. When he spoke he sounded upset.

'Would you mind telling me just what the fuck you're doing now,' he said.

'Hey, now wait a minute, this wasn't us.'

Cargill pointed at John and silenced him with a gloved forefinger placed across his own lips. Responding to the speed and anger of the gesture, John lowered his voice to nothing.

Cargill focused on Laura. They existed without the fires, the crew, the bystanders or John. He swallowed and blinked.

He turned away and sighed. She could tell he wanted to like her. She thought he was going to cuff her face as he raised his gloved hand, but he placed it on her shoulder.

'I don't know if you meant it, but it's your fault,' said Cargill. 'You've been here two days. Two days, and you've turned this poor man's fucked-up life upside down again. What did I tell you?'

'It wasn't me.'

'It was.'

The driver revved the pump hard. Shallow whirlpools formed in the water's surface. Hollow vacuumed hammering preceded a fullness of sound as impellers pressured extracted water into the hose. It writhed as it swelled, becoming turgid as air and spume hissed from the nozzle. The fully charged hose jolted the crew sideways.

'Hose charged sir.'

'Well put them out, for God's sake,' said Cargill, leaving Laura and John alone as he went to supervise, 'and spray the trees, don't let the whole hillside go up.'

'Yes, sir.'

She watched in a state of dreamlike detachment. The fire-fighters turned work into a target game, akin to the pistol ranges at the travelling fair, hooting as the power of their jet blasted the remains of the hives apart as they swept them away. Their aim was good and their fun was short-lived. The steam, emerging like the ghost of the fire to replace the smoke, robbed the night of its false light and warmth. Embers sizzled on the ground. A damp smell of destruction hung over the garden. The fall of myriad droplets created an eerie soundtrack as everything in the garden took on a sour tang, a taste that made Laura want to spit. A melancholy air settled on the crew, drained of adrenalin, splashing between the hive stands, extinguishing the remaining hot-spots, talking about Luther. Over at the main road, the spectators got back in their cars and drove away, the show over. When he was happy there was no longer any danger, Cargill called it a night. As his crew uncoupled the lengths of hose, emptied them of water and rolled them up, Cargill strolled over to Luther's house. The windows lit up. He crossed over them once each as he searched. It sounded hollow beneath his footfall. Turning the lights off, he came out and cut across to Laura and John, who hadn't moved. Producing a brilliant white handkerchief from inside his dirty tunic like a magician, he offered it to her. It was only then that she realised she was crying.

'Thank you.' She wiped the tears from her face.

'For what it's worth,' said Cargill, 'I think you're the catalyst more than the cause. It's been coming.'

'Since when?' said John, a little too quickly, as though this was something else he had kept from them when selling the house. Cargill ignored John but answered his question, directing it to Laura.

'Since Ishbel died, since Tarragh left, since he looked right through us all, that Sunday in the church.'

'You can't be serious?'

'I'd like you to tell me why not.' Cargill absorbed John's challenge until it dulled.

'I don't understand. Where is he? What's happening?' said Laura.

He turned back to Laura.

'I don't know. Why would he do this?'

Cargill scuffed the heels of his Wellingtons through the slushy ground as he walked away, leaving Laura staring into

Luther's garden, devoid of activity. In the stillness, the wet rows of charred wood caught the moonlight and the ground shone like a raven's wing. It was as quiet as a graveyard. She wiped her face again.

'Come on.' John put his arm around her and she allowed herself to be led back home.

Run-off trickled from Luther's land, crossing the lane just beyond their gate, making its way back to the lochan, where the final piece of suction hose was being upended and drained prior to stowage. The slamming of the roller shutter doors of the lockers and the turning off of the blue lights indicated an end to the job. All the crew had mounted save Cargill, who leant against the front bumper and waited for them, legs crossed, his helmet cradled in his hands. When they stopped in front of him, he gestured for them to come even closer, going so far as to pull Laura right up to him so he didn't have to raise his voice above the noise of the engine.

'He came to see me this afternoon,' he said, looking at John, including him, 'left some paperwork. Your name's on the envelope, Mrs Payne. It's sealed. You should come over, both of you probably.'

Laura nodded.

'Okay, 'night then.' He stood to go. 'I do regret what I did, J.P., I hope your wife passed that on to you.'

'She tried.'

'Maybe if I'd been more neighbourly…' he glanced from them to Luther's place, 'Well, who knows?'

The moment Cargill's door slammed, the driver selected drive and they pulled away, revealing Frank, sitting in an outside chair, his bad foot resting on another, a bottle of wine in his hand.

'Surprise.' He held what was left of the wine up to them. 'That was some show.'

'Frank?' said John. 'What are you doing here?'

'Signed myself out.'

'Is that wise?'

John sat next to Frank, trying to see the damage to his foot.

'You're kidding?' said Frank. 'It's got to be better than spending the night in a room full of dry cunts and numb nuts. Fuck, I might as well be dead. Remind me to tell Molly she can never put her Uncle Frank in a home.' He took a drink from the wine bottle. 'Besides, that fucker shot me. Can't let that go.'

'How long you been here?'

'Don't know, half an hour maybe.'

'You check Molly?' asked Laura.

'No, why? Should I?'

'No,' John pushed Frank back into his chair, 'you rest your foot, I'll go.'

'I'll go,' said Laura, glad of the chance to get away. As bad as she felt, Frank made it worse. She was going in when he called after her.

'Laura, tell me you've got some painkillers.'

She didn't answer.

Molly hadn't moved. She didn't need comforted, tucked in, unravelled or her hair pulled off her face. Laura needed them all.

From the landing, down the stairs and through the sunroom Laura heard John and Frank speculating, trying to rationalise what had happened. She extended her absence by escaping into the kitchen, looking for paracetamol. She slammed a cupboard shut, suddenly convinced that Frank had set fire to the hives. It was just the kind of vindictive shit he would get up to, letting everybody know Luther hadn't won. This conviction was challenged immediately by the sight of a cured leg of ham in the kitchen, hanging from the stainless steel pan rack in the far corner. She steadied herself against the back of the stool she had been sitting on at the start of the evening, when they had first smelled the smoke. She looked over her shoulder as she tiptoed to the meat; cast a glance down the dining room, hoping he was still there, waiting for her.

She lifted the cover over the thigh. In the dried surface of the meat was a pale indentation where the shaving she had tasted had once been. Poking out from the cloth, higher up the joint, was a torn yellow corner of paper, the size of a post-it note. Sliding it out she read the words 'trust me' in black pen. At the sound of John's approach she thrust it into her pocket and skipped over to the cupboard above the fridge. She pulled the tablets out and held them out to John as he came in.

'I hadn't forgotten.'

'No,' he said, 'didn't think you had. I'm just in for a beer. The wine's going down like water.' He popped a top and took half the bottle in one go. 'I think I should quench my thirst first, don't you think?'

'Try water, take a beer through.'

He drank a pint of tap water before popping the lids from two beers.

'John, take it easy, please.'

'Don't worry. I'm here to keep him out of any more trouble.' He kissed her on the forehead. 'And tomorrow's his last day. Can you be nice for one more night?'

'If he can.'

John hesitated, but he knew there was no answer that didn't depend upon Frank's behaviour.

'Okay, do your best, for me. I'm yours for the rest of the year.'

Outside, Laura accepted some wine from the bottle Frank had been drinking from, though she used a glass, making a promise to herself to cut right down on the drink as soon as Frank was gone. This thought alone allowed the tension to decant as the bottle was emptied. John hadn't eaten since lunch-time and the wine Frank kept topping him up with went straight to his head. He started with the twitch almost immediately. It looked like she'd be the one taking Frank to the airport so Laura paced herself, topping her own wine up with soda, until that was all she drank.

Frank protested his innocence when Laura asked if he'd set fire to Luther's hives, claiming he couldn't have done it with his foot like it was, conveniently forgetting that he'd made his way back to the house.

'Something needs to be done though.'

John agreed.

Frank made the most of his supposed immobility, playing up the wounded soldier routine and Laura did her bit; offering to get fresh wine from the fridge, seeing the sideways glances between the boys when she brought in crisps, nuts and olives, surprised at her amiability; feeling the appreciative squeeze on her knee from John, to let her know he knew she was making an effort. She kept them out of the kitchen all night.

Talk of what Frank was going to do to Luther became less

violent and more comic as they both became fixated on the image of him standing in front of them naked, as though it was the done thing. It got ridiculous. When John fell off his chair laughing, he knew his night was over. He stumbled off to bed, leaving Laura alone with Frank.

'Nice way to end a shitty day,' he said.

'Mmm, didn't expect this,' she said, trying to keep up the pretence. 'Can't say the Highlands are dull, can we?'

'Not at all.' Frank turned his attention from her to the outer dark that surrounded them. 'Where do you think he is?

She followed his gaze.

'Luther? I don't know.'

'I do.' She flinched. Frank was grinning at her, enjoying her response. 'He's out there, somewhere, watching; watching you. And who could blame him?'

However close or far away he was, if he was watching, Laura didn't mind. It was the way Frank looked at her that made her uncomfortable. She started scraping the remains of the snacks into one bowl and stacking them. Frank put his hand over hers.

'Here, I'll get the dishes.'

'Don't be silly.' She slid her hands from under his and lifted the bowls. 'Besides – your foot. It'll only take a minute.'

'If you insist.'

He sat back as she leant over for the cutlery, taking the chance for a quick look down her top.

He laughed to himself when she came back out for the glasses wearing a fleece.

'Feeling the cold?'

'A bit.' Gathering the glasses she put her hand on his. 'You finished?'

'No, but you can take the glass,' he said, lifting the almost empty bottle from the table and giving it a shake, 'I'll have one more for the ditch.'

From the kitchen Laura heard him grunting. Peeping around the corner she saw Frank stand up, get his balance as he tried his foot and hobble a few steps away from his chair. Holding the bottle by the neck he hurled it towards the lochan, shouting 'fuck you' as it spun in the air, giving the finger to the splash. She stood back, not wanting him to see her if he turned around. She stacked the dishwasher and put it on, even though it was only half-full. After she heard him come in the porch, she waited a few seconds before peering around the corner. The sunroom was clear.

'Thank fuck.'

Laura unzipped the fleece and threw it onto the breakfast counter.

Too wired for sleep, she poured herself a drink. She noticed the cured meat as she closed the fridge door. Taking a knife from the rack she tried to shave a wafer of meat off, the way he had. The resinous flesh pared away like candle wax. The taste brought Luther to mind; their first strange meeting, when he knew everything. She knew he was out there and she felt safe. Turning the lights out as she passed through the kitchen she took her drink into the snug.

Sitting back, she closed her eyes and nestled her head in the back cushion of the sofa.

The downstairs toilet flushed.

She was leaning across to turn the table lamp off when Frank filled the doorway.

'I thought you were going to bed.'

'Mm, so did I,' he said.

His leg rubbed against hers as he sank into the sofa next to her, penning her in between him and the arm. He leant closer, his breath stinking of drink.

'Sorry I give you a hard time sometimes,' he said. 'About that stuff, you know, the past. I just don't like to see him hurt.'

'You're the one hurting him; stop bringing it up.'

'You're right, Laura, you're right. I can't get it out of my head. It's my problem.'

Frank gripped her neck, pulled her around to face him and kissed her. She pushed him away and put some space between them.

'You're drunk, Frank, go to bed.'

'Come on, you've done it before.'

'It's not a mistake I intend making again.' Laura jumped up from the couch. He stood at the same time and moved to put himself between her and the door.

'Come on,' he said, moving towards her, resting his weight on his good leg. 'I've seen the way you've been looking at me. A bit of you wants to.' She slapped his hands away as she stepped backwards. 'Let's just see.'

'Frank, stop it. This isn't funny.' Turning her back on him she was looking through the window into the kitchen, where the paring knife she had just used lay next to the sink. She cringed, pulling her arms tight into her chest as he came up behind her and put his chin on her shoulder. He spoke to her reflection, his tone heavy and taunting.

'You've done it before.'

'No.'

She fought for her breath as he grabbed her from behind, the palm of his hand over her mouth, her nose held closed between his thumb and forefinger, forcing her against the window. A blade flashed across the glass as it sprung open.

'Done it before, Laura.' She was dizzy, struggling to breathe when she felt the cold of the tip push against her neck. He placed it right on top of her scar. It was exactly the same. The hand, the knife, the pressure in her back, and all she could think about is that she should have known; Frank was just the kind of arsehole that would have a switchblade. She tried to scream into his muffling hand, only stopping when he intensified the pressure over her mouth, arching her neck back. He pressed with the blade; his lips brushing her ears as he spoke.

'I'll cut you again,' closer to her ear, 'trust me.' She started to panic. He put his knees into the back of hers and leant against her as she slid down the wall, dumped to the floor. His fingers raked her hair into a handle, pulling at the roots. The blade floated in the air right next to her, too close for her to bring it into focus.

'Come on,' he said, unzipping. 'Was it really that bad?'

Frank yanked her head around, causing her to cry out. He forced himself into her open mouth. When Laura tried to bite through him he pushed harder, into her throat. She recoiled from the gag reflex, thrashing her head from side to side; her teeth sawing against him, until she felt the knife against her nose.

'Spite your face, Laura?'

She stopped.

Tears stung her eyes and her face burned as she eased the pressure.

Upstairs, a floorboard creaked. Frank froze. He gripped her hair even tighter.

'Not a fucking word, you hear? Just think about Molly.'

John's unsteady steps lumbered above them. A brief silence was followed by the jet of his urine piercing the water. The chain flushed. He stumbled back to bed without washing his hands.

Frank carried on, relaxing his grip. It wasn't long before she felt him spurt into her. A shallow moan accompanied his discharge, followed by his bending double to swing a boxer's punch into her diaphragm, causing her to spume his come back onto him. He re-tightened his hand around the fist of hair, tilting her backwards as he grinned down, forcing her to look at him as he shrank inside her; dragging his taste across her tongue. He rubbed the point of the blade against her windpipe causing her to swallow.

'Nice try, Laura.'

He withdrew.

'He'll kill you,' she said.

Frank laughed and he stroked her face as though he felt sorry for her.

'You're damaged goods,' he said, standing up straight. 'John could only forgive you once you'd been punished.' He dragged the knife up her throat, tracing her chin and her lips before pushing the tip into a nostril. 'Do you think you have?'

'Don't.'

'See,' he said, folding the knife, 'I'm not all bad. People don't appreciate my good side, even John. I set him free and he's never thanked me. You want to play some more?'

'Get off me, Frank.'

'Well, if you're not game,' he said, letting her hair unravel from his grip as he moved away, 'I'm away to my bed. Night.'

He took a final look from the doorway and winked.

'Under your own roof, how does that make you feel?'

He was gone by the time she vomited into the paper bin.

Luther saw Frank pulling his zip up as he came out of the old Macpherson place. The thought of her going with both of them scorched his mind. The burst of relief he felt when he saw her hunched over a bin, spitting it out, rejecting it, shamed him. Her hair fell about her head in ratty tails and he knew she'd been held. His shame fuelled the anger that no longer smouldered like a heath fire, below the surface, making it impossible for him not to act or wait any longer.

Through the door, in the scant patch of light afforded by the lamp, he watched, privy to a black moment, as she held herself up on straight arms, the same way Tarragh had in the early stages of her pregnancy, when morning sickness had bent her double for the first three months. She had been weakened by the experience and had cried often. The sobs that shook Laura as she brought up another flapping string of bile now made a happy ending unlikely for any of them.

He watched her as she dry-heaved a couple of times. With nothing left to bring up, she sat back on her heels, pushed her hair from her face and got rid of the tears with the heel of her hand. Even though he knew he wasn't visible, her stare found him. Direct and unbroken, it cut through the space between them and pulled him out of hiding. Side-lit by the security light from the porch he approached the house, his half-reflection growing on the outside of the sunroom wall until it stood within the doorway of weak light that contained Laura, like the night quarters of a captive animal. She turned off the table lamp, leant forward and pushed the door. It swung into its frame and she was gone. Luther turned away, unable to face himself.

The smell from the bin made her gag. It was overpowering, even though she had pushed it away, into the space behind the door. The stench filled the room, a solid presence pushing her back and down into the corner beneath the faint fan of light that came through the window from the kitchen.

Laura sucked air through chattering teeth. A slime of cold sick-sweat chilled her and she wanted nothing more than to stand beneath the scalding spray of a shower. But the showers were upstairs. The thought of him lying up there appalled her. She had no idea what life would be like in the morning. All she knew was that it had changed. Crawling from her corner she pulled her fleece from the sofa and put it on, zipping it up to her neck. Taking a deep breath she retrieved the bin, opened the door and put it out of sight in the sunroom. He was gone. Rabbits nibbled at the lawn.

Using garden wire, Luther circled their necks and limbs to bind them together. Once bound, he formed a hook with the free end and suspended the bundle of soft toys from the light fitting above her bed.

His movement through the house had been deliberate yet soundless. The new floor was well-laid and all he'd had to remember was to avoid the fifth step on the stairway, knowing this to be the only one that creaked.

He knelt beside her like one at prayer, in thrall to the shallow breathing of deep sleep. Forcing the tremble from his hands he pushed the quilt around and beneath her in a duck down cocoon. Wrapped in his arms, with her head supported by one hand, Molly was taken from her bed. Before leaving the room, Luther used his old Zippo to light the end of a piece of waxed string trailing from the toy bundle.

Luther paused in the porch looking back down the length of the house. The entrance to the old Macpherson place remained closed. He imagined her crammed into a lightless corner, trying to stay out of sight. He couldn't be sure any comfort he might offer now would be accepted. The look on her face had expressed disappointment, if not blame. Did she think he had seen, watched, or that he had taken any pleasure in it? Besides, any such comfort would be short-lived. His real work tonight would be of long-term benefit to mother and child. He was saving them. He chewed a few more painkillers.

Carrying the child with a natural tenderness, her cheek resting on his shoulders, the pressure parting her lips, he took Molly's whispered breath against his ear as both a miracle and confirmation that he was doing the right thing. Had she woken, he would have stopped. Her weight in his arms, the curls of her hair tickling his chin, the sweetness of her breath, all became ensnared in the triggered memories of Ishbel, whose legs always hung loose, swaying with his step, bare feet that were never cold. He missed the trust of arms around his neck.

They were nearing his home when the smoke alarm went off.

Luther's home was like an oven. The loaded Rayburn would have been hot enough to cope with the severest of winter's nights. Tonight the heat it generated was physically oppressive, forcing Luther to stoop as he went to the rear. He used his foot to open the door and slipped into the comparative cool of his bedroom. He lay Molly down on the half of the bed he slept on. When he was sure she was still sound, he closed the door to maintain the temperature, went outside and sat in his Defender, waiting.

The roof windows of the new house opened and a black cloud burst forth like a cave's evening release of bats. It wasn't long before the upstairs window of the child's bedroom flew open and a ball of stuffed flames fell to the garden. He turned the ignition, revved the engine hard and waited for them to appear. The moment he saw them he tore away from his home, driving as fast as he could or had ever done on the track that led to Milton, disappearing into the trees.

Laura had started awake and instinctively pushed back from everything, crouching in the snug corner watching the door, wishing she had gone to the kitchen for the knife. She waited for Frank. The alarm that rattled the house and her mind had to be some more of his twisted shit. But the door didn't open; swearing, panic in the running footsteps above and the sound of John screaming Molly's name woke her to the fact that something was wrong and forced her out of hiding.

The acrid smell of burning chemicals filled her nose as she ran upstairs. By the time she reached the top she was choking. John was stooped, leaning against the wall, retching as the dense, toxic smoke sank from the ceiling, filling the corridor.

'The controls, push the controls?' John shouted at her, pointing up at the glass ridge. As she pushed the button to open the roof, Frank burst out of the bathroom and along the corridor with a dripping towel, calling over his shoulder.

'John, come on, now.'

Beyond them, night light horses galloped around the burning sun that lit Molly's room, gobbets of flaming plastic falling on an empty bed.

Molly?

Molly?

Molly?

The absence screamed at her as Frank and John jumped onto the bed and smothered the flames with the towel.

The sun went out.

John yelped with pain as he unhooked the boiling globe from the destroyed lampshade. Jumping from the bed, they threw it through the open window, where the towel fell away and it re-ignited, falling like a meteor eating through the atmosphere.

'Molly Molly, it's mummy, Molly. Please, Molly, it's okay.'

John leapt back over the bed holding his hand and rushed into the bathroom.

Laura was on all fours, scouring the bedroom, ripping the sheets off, under the bed, in the wardrobe, in drawers, when she remembered the cot and laughed with relief. Looking up she was face to face with Frank.

'John.'

He slapped her hard, grabbed her head and pulled her close, forcing his words into her ear, 'Not a fucking word, you hear, not a fucking word.'

The cot was empty. She reared away, screaming and lunged at Frank, slapping, scratching, howling, punching, 'This is you, fucking you, this is all your fault, what have you done with her, why are you doing this to me, why, why, why?'

John ran from the bathroom, a wet flannel wrapped around his injured palm. He pulled Laura back from her frenzied attack, trying to hold her, restrain her and comfort her all at the same time, shaking his head at Frank in an, 'I'm fucking sorry about this man,' manner that, even in that moment, she at least found a seed of comfort in. He didn't know. He couldn't. He would help her, surely.

'Laura – Laura – stop this shit, come on,' he held her tight, kissed her on the temple. 'Please, you need to help us find Molly.'

They all heard a diesel engine at full throttle. John let go of Laura.

'FUUUUUUCK,' he screamed from the window. 'He's got her. Look.' John gripped Frank by the shoulder, forcing him to look outside. They knocked her out of the way as they hurdled over the bed. Frank threw a sly punch as he followed John out.

Blue moonlight horses continued their gallop.

Blood dripped from her top lip as they spewed out of the driveway in the truck, swerving and rutting until she saw their tail-lights disappear.

The instant they did, Luther's Defender rumbled into view beyond his house, emerging from the forest, blacker than shadow, defined by its edges, creeping between the trees and the ruined hives, to come to a stop, mostly hidden, alongside his back door. The lights of the house went on as he moved through it. Moments later, he stepped out of the front door of his house. In the brief time he was silhouetted by his kitchen bulb, she could see he was carrying a bundle that could only be Molly. Laura ran downstairs to meet him.

She ran the length of the sunroom as Luther stepped out

of the porch. The instant he saw her he formed a shield with his whole body to protect the child. The knife went into his shoulder. Leaving it embedded, Laura staggered backwards, horrified, not believing how she had done it. She watched Luther unfurl, like a hedgehog sensing the danger was over, groaning as he tried to move his arm.

'You'll need to take it out,' he said, craning his neck to see the knife. 'I've got things I need to do.'

Rooted to the spot, Laura shook from head to toe, her left hand clamped around her right as she chewed at what remained of her pinky nail.

'Laura. Please.'

'What are you doing?' she said, uncertain steps taking her closer to him.

'I'm bringing the baby back.'

'But,' Laura said, 'Why did you take her?'

'Baby needs her mum, mum needs her baby. I'm no good.'

Her hand trembled as it wrapped around the handle causing him to cry out through clenched teeth. She pulled back.

'I can't.'

'Just do it quickly,' he said, 'without thinking, straight out, the way it went in.'

The knife came out with little resistance, separating from the bone, sucking through muscle. Blood seeped from the stab as he moved his arm, staining his shirt. She dropped the knife at her feet.

'I should put her down.'

Laura gestured to the snug.

Luther bowed his head as he entered, dropped to his knees and as if by slight of hand, Molly was lying on the sofa, multi-coddled in her quilt and a rabbit fur wrap.

'She's been asleep all the time,' said Luther. 'You could put her back in bed and she wouldn't know anything had happened.'

'She has no bed.'

'True.'

She put her hand on his shoulder, her index finger slipping through the slice in his shirt. She could feel the incision, warm and viscous across her fingertip.

'Does it hurt?' she said.

'Yes.'

'What are you trying to do to me?'

'Nothing.'

'Then why did you take her?'

'Teach him a lesson; show him what he's got.'

'He knows.'

'He hits you, both. He'll lose it all.'

Luther's face displayed every day and memory of his life as he looked down at Molly. He touched her forehead with his and inhaled as though she was the last fragrance. When he looked back to Laura he was close to tears. 'I'm sorry.' He laughed. 'I'm not doing this for you. I'm not even doing this for her.' He wiped his sleeve across his face. 'I don't like him and I'm trying to help him. Figure that out. Will he be helped?'

'I think so,' said Laura. 'Where is he?'

'Close.'

Luther could see the truck. It would be impaled upon the sharpened trunk he'd embedded in the track, fan shattered, radiator bleeding, airbags deflating, progress halted. The wire they'd released ten yards previous would be drifting through the headlights like a broken trout line, snagged and snapped on the rock the angler didn't see, didn't anticipate. Stunned as they would be, both men, if they survived, would get out and move away for fear of fuel leakage and explosion. They would realise that Luther could not have got past the trap, that he had fooled them, was behind them. They would be angry. They would be ten minutes away. That left him with five.

Laura was transfixed by the sight of his blood dripping and soaking into the carpet. She knew that this was the first bad thing to happen in this room, she knew this and she didn't want it to be. She used her fleece to catch the blood, to stop it soaking into the carpet, through to the stone; she wanted it away, gone, not part of the history. But it was. The first stain was her fault. The blood ran down his thumb and pooled on to the fleece. His sleeve was soaked.

'I asked you to trust me: you couldn't. You had doubts.'

Laura nodded, unsure what to think when it was evident he was pleased with her response.

'I didn't know it was you, couldn't be sure,' she said. 'Frank said the words; 'trust me'. It could have been him.'

'That's good,' he said as he stood. 'Molly needs you to doubt.'

Instinctively, Laura leant to kiss Luther, but pulled away, repulsed as she remembered Frank. She grabbed his wrist, light-headed. His raised hands came to rest either side of her face and held her, fragile and precious. She felt he was holding her up. He leant to her and he kissed her on the top of the head, little more than a peck, no more than a goodbye.

As she looked up, his eyes were dimmer, sadder, no longer exploring, content with the surface.

'I need to go.'

'Why? Please stay.'

'Look at us,' he said. 'You're crying. I'm bleeding.'

'I'll fix your wound.'

His blood mixed with her tears as he tried to wipe them away, smudging and smearing until he resorted to the cuff of his clean sleeve to absorb everything.

'I'll see to it. Besides, I haven't finished.'

She smiled as he used a spot of spittle on the shirt to enable him to take the last trace of them from her cheek.

'Sorry,' he said. 'I should have asked. Impulse, I suppose, even after all this time.'

'It's okay.'

'I used to hate it when my mum did it to me.'

'I think every child does.'

She wanted him to kiss her again and knew that he wouldn't; he was already somewhere else, with someone else. The stare that had skewered her on their first meeting was gone. He was inside himself. Her skin tingled as the back of his knuckles traced her jaw-line. The corner of a smile played across his face and she wondered what memory was playing.

'Do you want him back?'

Unexpected as the question was she had no hesitation in answering 'Yes' and was angered by how reassured this made her feel.

'What about the other one: who was supposed to be in hospital?'

'You're giving me the choice?' she said, half of her taking him seriously.

'Yes.'

It was the flat, serious intonation. He was giving her the opportunity to be part of whatever it was he had started. She didn't shake, go cold, get a dry throat, develop a twitch or feel the weight of the decision pressing down on her shoulders. She took her chance.

'I don't care if I never see him again.'

'Why?'

'You know why.'

'I don't. I didn't see. But I can guess. Does he know? Your husband?'

'No, John doesn't know.'

'No doubts?'

His arms dropped to his side and he was once again looking at her. She knew he could see her doubt but she insisted.

'I'm sure.'

'Fine,' he said, though she could tell he was disappointed. 'You can have him back.'

'Luther, you don't know me well enough to judge me.'

Choosing not to respond, he turned away. Leaning over Molly he used a finger to move a curl away from her mouth, grinning broadly at the delayed reaction of her face responding to the tickling.

'Bye, darling.'

When he straightened she could tell their time was over. He gripped her by the shoulder with his good arm.

'You're better than him. You deserve more; she deserves more. We're no good.'

'Will John be okay?'

'Why? Are you going to be here for him?'

She nodded.

Luther sighed.

'You're the strong one. You being here is more important than him coming back.'

'I want him.'

Letting go, he left the room without looking back.

Luther lifted the cover of the Rayburn and laid the half-full jerrican on the hotplate. Opening the door he threw some more logs in. He turned all the lights off, except the one which hung above the stairwell, and went downstairs to wait for their arrival.

He'd expected to wait longer. The crash of the door and the screaming of his name suggested they were less injured than he had anticipated; they were on his trail, baying for his life. After all, John was searching for his missing daughter. From his position in the entrance to the passage, he could see back across the cellar to where he'd placed Molly's shoe on the floor, in the small pool of light at the bottom of the stairs.

When John's shadow fell across the shoe, it was Luther's cue to move.

Without rushing, he made good ground as he followed the beam of his head-torch along the well-worn route, all the time listening for their progress behind him. He was encouraged to hear their thunderous descent down the wooden staircase, Frank noticeably limping; relieved at John's shock as he lifted the shoe, releasing the final wire, followed closely by the crack of the trapdoor slamming above them, trapping the darkness. What they couldn't know, as they blundered about, cursing and swearing, hands outstretched, searching the walls, recoiling from anything sharp or furry, shouting at each other to find the switch, to go back up the stairs, was that the closure of the trapdoor was final. The internal handle rattled against its screws in Luther's pocket as he walked. They had to follow. After about a hundred yards, Luther stopped to listen. Sound carried along the relatively straight trajectory of the tunnel to this point. Frank found the light switch, but only after cutting himself on the keen edge of the axe. His banging against the door stopped as soon as John found the passage and realised they had been trapped. Luther heard him call Frank over and pictured them standing at the entrance, wondering if he was in there, how far it went, where it came out, if he had Molly. They had no choice. He recognised the sound of each tool as they snatched them from the racks, describing them as weapons. The instructions from John, explaining to Frank how to prime them, meant they were lighting the Tilley lamps Luther had prepared. They left the cellar and moved quickly. Luther turned his torch off and waited for the glow of their lamps to show, like some subterranean sunrise. He wanted them to hear him ahead of them.

When the jerrican blew, Luther knew his house no longer existed. It exploded with a violence that shook the stone around him and in the immediate aftermath shrunk the world into a pocket of silence that contained him and them on opposite sides. The rush of hot air and dust that blasted past told him that the trapdoor had been blown in. The growing roar contained echoes of smashing glass and falling crockery. It was a burning past, collapsing with no one to bear witness, to stand amongst it and make sure.

He waited to hear if they'd survived. Within seconds there

was coughing, checking and reassuring as they gathered themselves: the scuffing of feet and the strain of exertion. It sounded like one of them at least had been knocked off his feet; Frank probably, already without the full use of one of his legs. They didn't hang around. When their light appeared Luther ran for the cavern, making no attempt to soften his footfall, his familiarity with the way enabling him to put distance between him and their reanimated curses and threats.

At the fork, where the floor sloped down to the right he felt the rise in temperature. This time it came from ahead. The left hand fork rose before it dipped to the cavern. Luther felt the lining of his nose desiccating as he continued through the burning air to duck through the entrance.

Inside the cavern, Luther could see that the burning had passed its peak. The firepit resembled a stalled magma flow, a rolling boil of red and orange heart-wood that pulsated as its remaining energy was given up. Brittle pinking had replaced the oxygen-fuelled volley of cracks and snaps from blazing logs. Heat-distorted air swirled within the chamber, liquefying golden walls that glittered and sparkled with glassy reflections of sun-bright light. Old Callum's pipes, lying in state in their box, shimmered like the ancient fleece sought by the Argonauts, each white thread of their tartan weave turned precious. Tarragh's face was alive with movement, complex expressions passing over her face in communion with the mood of the fire. He prickled all over with sweat.

Luther took Molly's other shoe from his pocket. He placed it on the floor where it would be the first thing seen. The longer he waited the calmer he became. It was all in place. Everything he would ever need was here.

Before long he heard them stop at the fork. Upon investigation, neither of them thought they should take the right tunnel, or tunnels, as they discovered. They didn't know what to make of the rising temperature, or the strange orange glow that met them as they looked down the final stretch of the passageway. He could hear their breathing.

'Looks like we're here,' said John.

'It's like the door to an oven.'

'Not what I was thinking.'

'Fuck, John,' said Frank, 'you don't think he's the devil, do you?'

'Whoever he is, he's here and he's got Molly.'

Luther took a firm grip of the axe handle leaning alongside the opening.

John came out on all fours, so low did he have to bend to get through. He reached out. The fingers of his right hand wrapped around the shoe. Before he had a chance to raise his head, Luther sapped it with the club the way he would still a trout with a priest. John fell into the cavern, face down, out cold. His Tilley lamp crashed to the floor. Luther dropped the club and lifted his rifle.

'John. John, what the...'

Frank took a bullet in the back of his neck, where his spine met the base of his skull.

For the time being, Luther left Frank where he fell, needing to deal with John while he was still unconscious. He heaved John into position, sitting upright, his hands pulled behind his back and tied around the stake Luther had driven into a fissure in the stone floor. Using gaffer tape to bind John's head to the stake, he made it so that he could only see in one direction, the wall ahead. He gaffered John's feet to either side of a log, in order to further immobilise him, but opted not to use a gag. This done, it was time to dispose of Frank.

His feet hadn't made it out of the passage. Luther walked over him, ducked in and took the Tilley to the top of the rise. Coming back down, he took a few moments before gripping the body by the ankles and dragging him up the slope. The effort reopened the stab wound in his shoulder. The pain was becoming harder to manage and he had to will the dizziness away. He refused to be too weak to finish it. Two minutes later he dropped the legs of the corpse onto the path. Moving to the side, he sat down with his back against the wall, sucking in deep breaths as his heart slowed. The cold stone helped numb his shoulder. Lifting his knees to his chest, he placed one foot on a hip and another in the oxter and straightened his legs. The body tumbled three or four times towards the impenetrable darkness of the right fork before it stopped, as though held by the light of the lamp. Shuffling down to it, Luther rested on his good arm and repeated his actions, kicking against the body with all the effort he could muster. It rolled a considerable distance and he guessed was still rolling when it could no longer be heard or seen.

Stars shone visibly through the crack in the passage ceiling; Orion's belt and sword, renamed O'Brian by Ishbel. He craned his neck to the clear night, wanting to see one last shooting star. Minutes passed. Sticking his fingers through the crack as far as the ball of his thumb, Luther felt the chill air and bent them to touch the damp bed of the stream edge. The waterfall sounded farther away than he knew it to be. More minutes: then the first note of the dawn chorus.

It took a conscious effort to release his grip and withdraw his fingers. Putting them to his nose he was convinced he could smell the imminent morning, rain in the air and fish in the pool. No shooting stars. He had to be satisfied with the constant orbit of the satellite that passed through his field of vision.

Clasping the slack line that hung through from the outside, he pulled until it was taut. Wrapping it three or four times around his stronger forearm he leant back and took the strain. It was a one-man tug of war. Keeping a constant tension in the line he inched his way backwards, grunting, grinding his teeth, not giving up, until the makeshift lever finally rolled the tree from the bank. It fell less than twelve inches yet its bulk dropped into the stream with such force that the crack disappeared. It was replaced by a triangular hole as a chunk of the roof fell in. In that instant, he could have climbed out, had he not slipped and fallen with the give in the line. Water began to pour in before he could get to his feet. Not the steady flow he had expected but a stream's worth, gushing through the hole in a solid column, sweeping him from his feet once more as it dragged him in its flow, backwards, into the right fork. It was all he could do to hold on. Turning his head away from the flow, water crashed against him, pummelling his neck and shoulders, testing muscle and tendon to the limit. It felt as though his arm would be pulled free of its socket. Forcing his chin into his chest he managed to breathe in the small pocket of air that the stream didn't steal on its downward journey. He faced down as he caught his breath. Water bounced bright from his toes and was gone, swallowed by the depths. Frank would never be found.

One

Two

Three

He rolled onto his stomach, raised his head and tried to make himself as streamlined as possible. The Tilley burned bright beyond the fall of water. Invigorated by the challenge, driven by adrenaline and the knowledge of a job unfinished, Luther worked his way up the line, fighting the flow, towards the curtain of water that fell in from the sky.

His deliverance through to the other side was cause for quasi-religious rejoicing as he laughed and slapped the dry floor.

'Frank?'

Luther turned to the cavern. How long had John been shouting?

He squelched back down the slope into the oven-like heat of the cavern to stand before John. Water and blood marked his trail. Steam rose from his head and clothes. John ceased his struggling as Luther approached. His legs lay limp on the floor. His voice was robbed of its strength.

'Where's Frank?'

'Gone.'

John's eyes were wild with panic, straining from their sockets to see behind Luther, who stepped aside, so he could see the entrance, and the wall, where their two Tilleys sat on the floor next to a canvas hunting bag, the club and the rifle.

'Frank. Frank.'

There was no answer.

'Where is he? He wouldn't leave me here. What have you done with him?'

'I killed him.' Luther didn't elaborate this blunt, unapologetic statement of fact as he turned the lamps out and retrieved the rifle and his bag. Without the harsh light of the lamps the walls once again took on the pulsating glow of the firepit.

'I don't believe you.'

'Then where is he?'

Luther knew, when he came back to crouch in front of his captive, that he had changed. He was tiring. The heat, the wound and recent exertions were taking their toll. He imagined his smile was laced with something approaching pity as he tapped the man gently on the arm.

'I'm here to help,' he said, 'to clarify things.'

Taking his whisky from the bag, he twisted the cork out, took a good slug and offered the bottle to John's lips.

'Listen to that,' said Luther, looking over his shoulder. They listened to the cascade crashing into the tunnel, the volume and the rhythm of the descent coming to the fore. 'That's the stream that turns the wheel in Milton, your little dream town. It's just about to stop. A dam is forcing the waters in. A dam I made. They're draining away, plunging farther down the cave system than I've ever been.' He illustrated the drop of the water by closing his fingers and diving his hand into his bag. When he withdrew it he popped a few tablets into his mouth, chewing them briefly before going on. 'A long time ago, I went in search of a dog called Bheag. I don't know how long I was down there, how far I got; but I couldn't get to the bottom. If there is one, that's where your brother is being flushed to. Eventually, he'll lie with the bones of Bheag: poor company for a good dog. Best you forget about him.'

John spat his whisky at Luther. Luther didn't react beyond closing his eyes against the stinging. The drink shone as it ran around the contours of his mouth, blending with sweat before catching the golden light fully as it dripped from his chin.

'I killed him for raping Laura.'

Denial flashed across John's face and he tried to shake his head within the constraints of the tape binding. Luther's unbroken stare as he watched John struggle was enough to cause a flicker of doubt to breach the anger of John's disbelief.

'While you were upstairs, asleep, drunk.'

John's doubt was compounded by the realisation that it could be true, he couldn't deny it. His troubled features lost their strength.

'Now you know.'

Luther stood. The fire cast his shadow up the arching cinema screen of the wall, a weary silhouette cast by the evening sun in the west, a long day beaten. 'Listen to the water and know that you're better off. If you were to ask me, I'd suggest you use this new knowledge to help deal with the loss. I know about loss.'

His shadow took wings and swept over the ceiling of the cavern, losing its intensity as he left the man behind, before coalescing back into a gargoyle of a smudge, identifiable only by his movement, as he sat down between the man and the firepit, with Tarragh by his side.

The bowl they shared, the stone coracle, polished by the swirl of ancient, underground eddies, was comfortable in its warmth and smoothness. Luther took his shirt off. Sweat-soaked and tacky with blood, it peeled away from his wound without much in the way of fresh pain. He balled it and tossed it behind him. It sizzled before bursting into flames, adding yellow to the redness of the air. He did the same with his boots.

In front of him, John had the demeanour of a rag doll and it appeared that the restraining stake was now holding him up. Was that a sob? Luther guessed he was seeing his brother defiling his wife, his wife being defiled by his brother. Was he trying to dismiss the multiple scenarios flooding his mind, some involving pleasure: on his brother's face, their faces, hers only, or neither as his brother wept or his wife tried to scream, held down against her will? Such imagination was an ugly place to be, one with no permanent escape.

All Luther had in the bag was whisky, a knife and the medication from Ali Shah. He filled his mouth with painkillers before taking the cork from the whisky and flipping it backwards. He gulped from the bottle, clearing his mouth with a quarter of the contents. He stood, unbuckled his belt and stepped from his combats when they fell around his ankles. They went the same way as his shirt. Sitting on the rear lip of the bowl, Luther sighed, a sign of relaxation rather than fatigue.

'That feels better, believe me.'

The man didn't respond.

'I sleep in a T-shirt. You know that? Never did; slept naked all the time, always too hot, I was a furnace. That's what she called me, her furnace. Ishbel was our wee hot pie. Outside I'm fine; a T-shirt's enough in winter, if you're doing something, keeping active. In bed though, can't generate my own heat anymore.' He drank some more. 'Warm in here though, hey? Like the waiting room to hell. Pretty though; like it used to be. No sleeping alone tonight.' Luther leant across and stroked Tarragh's head. 'Isn't that right, blossom?'

'Nooo,' screamed John. He kicked and bucked as he realised that the smaller smudge in the flames was another person.

'What's wrong? Have you suddenly remembered that you're looking for your daughter?'

'You leave her alone; you get your fucking hands off her.'

'You're in no position to be telling me what to do.'

'You keep away from her or so help me God I'll kill you, Luther.'

'She's dead. She can't hear you; she can't feel anything.' He drank some whisky. 'Do you suppose being dead is easy? It's the safest place to be though, don't you think? You can't be got when you're dead.'

Luther continued to stroke Tarragh's head. A few hairs dislodged and came away and stuck to his palm. They were lustrous, rich and held the sheen of polished brass so well that they could have come from the living head of the girl he couldn't save from himself. 'Look what you've done.' They were the last words she ever really heard. She never rejected or escaped their weight. She drank through the guilt rather than share it. When he took it back, the day he found her body, it had the weight of two deaths, both his fault. Life since that day had been his penance.

The man's screaming turned to howling. He was calling to Molly, thinking her dead. Her young name bounced around the small hot space like a lost soul looking for a way out. Luther hardly heard it as he rolled the filaments of hair between the tips of his thumb and forefinger, asking Tarragh for forgiveness, over and over, until she appeared before him, clear as day. There was no reading her face. He wanted her to be pleased to see him, happy for them to be back together. And then he knew why she couldn't be; they were incomplete. Ishbel lay alone. He dropped the hairs. She receded into the sunken cheeks and empty sockets he had coveted, leaving him hollow and hungry to be gone.

John's whining drifted into this emptiness. He couldn't tell if John had gone mad yet, but Luther wasn't enjoying the taunting the way he thought he would. After another slug from the bottle, he set it aside. Luther knelt beside Tarragh and pulled the Navajo rug tight around her.

'There you go,' he said, 'snug as a bug.'

He scooped her up into his arms and drew her close. A toe bone clicked as it fell to the floor. Unsteady steps took Luther once more to the front of the cavern where he stood above John, his genitals at eye level, holding the bundle across his chest, their combined shadow an unstable crucifix. John cracked. He started blubbing, snotty tears and high whiney words.

'What are you doing?'

Luther looked down.

'I want to show you something.'

Crouching again, so that John could see, Luther held Tarragh's remains out for him to look at. John was scared and forced his eyes tight closed against what he thought he would see.

'You need to look.'

His face shone with fluid. The skin of his forehead had split where he had struggled to free himself from the tape restraint. He was bleeding freely. Had he a free hand, Luther would have wiped him clean.

'Why are you doing this to me?' said John.

'I wanted to hurt you. I don't anymore. You need to look.'

John opened his eyes, slowly. It wasn't Molly.

'What is it?

'Her name was Tarragh. She's dead. Molly's fine.'

'Where?'

'At home, with her mum.'

'How do I know you're telling the truth?'

'I've just told you.' said Luther. He frowned, perturbed by the man's question. 'Why would I lie? Why would I hurt Molly?'

'I don't know. Thank you.'

'It's a life sentence, having a child. Even when they're with you, you can't protect them. There's never any peace. Look at her,' he said, shaking the mummy beneath the man's nose. 'This is what they can do to you, no matter how hard you try. If you forget them, for one single moment, they can destroy you. Are you strong enough to lose them? That's the only question, really.' Luther stood. 'I just want it to be over.'

With nothing else to say, he carried Tarragh back and laid her down; fitting her into the vessel's curved contours as though to make her comfortable and secure for the journey ahead. Swaying slightly, he rubbed his face hard, fighting fatigue and the blurred vision brought on by the drink, telling himself he was nearly finished.

'I need water,' said John.

Luther told himself he hadn't heard, held his breath, trying to pretend that John wasn't there any more.

'Please.'

Sighing, made conscious of his dry throat, the rills of sweat coursing down his body, Luther lifted the hunting bag and forced his body to do this one last thing.

When he stumbled back out of the passageway, fresh cuts to his head and knees, water slopped from the dripping bag, the handle gripped in one hand as he had used the other to negotiate the dark. He leant on the stake for balance as he retrieved the knife from the bag and sliced through the tape that restricted his captive's head. Once freed, John leant forward, slurping and sucking like a pit pony at its nose bag. Slaked, he leant back against the post. Luther poured the dregs over him, watching, with a drunk's fascination, as they ran through his hair, rinsed his face and percolated through his beard to dribble sunset-pink onto his chest in diamond-clear definition.

'What now?'

'Time to die,' said Luther, dropping the bag, keeping the knife, stumbling away.

With a final glance at the man newly met at the start of the weekend, Luther slipped into the space next to his wife. Resting the nape of his neck on the brim of their bowl he drained the whisky. The loose, loping arc of the bottle stopped where it crunched into the embers. His arms lay at his side, limp. Almost asleep, he had to force himself to act, in case sleep wasn't enough, in case he woke up. Concentration restored a field of vision that was practically in focus and allowed him to draw the blade across his left wrist with force and accuracy. There was no pain. Turning the handle, he jammed it into his mouth so that the edge faced outwards and presented his right wrist. He whipped his head sideways, scraping bone as he sliced through in a much less tidy procedure. A thick flap of skin hung loosely from the heel of his thumb. He dug his teeth into the leather grip until the pain became a throb. Assured of adequate blood loss, he lay back and let go.

On the cavern walls their tin-lid mobiles shone orange, mud bodies and hand-prints multiplied, mirror stars divided as they winked in conspiracy with the broken glass planets.

Everything spun to the wail of Old Callum's pipes. Slumping inward into the circle, his curved form faced Tarragh; two halves of a cooling locket.

When the house exploded, she knew they were dead. Luther hadn't delivered John back to her. Molly was without a father.

It was the evening of the next day before she was disabused of this notion, one she was already coming to terms with.

Cargill came to her door in his fire-fighter uniform; behind him the strobic blue lights of police cars and fire engines flashed over the remains of Luther's house. He informed her that John had been found alive, that they were bringing him out; she should get Molly and be ready to go with the ambulance. Looking old beyond his age and troubled beyond his experience, he had asked her permission to sit for a moment. Two deep breaths later, he took his hands away from his face.

'Can I get you a glass of water?' said Laura.

'That would be good, yes, thank you.'

Nerves caused the glass to rattle against the tap as she filled it. She took deep breaths and had to concentrate on not spilling any as she carried it to him. Cargill took a mouthful and nodded in appreciation. Standing, he walked outside, took his helmet off and poured the remains over his already soaked head. His hair ran tight against his skull and he looked cadaverous when he turned back to Laura.

'Is John okay?' she said.

'I would say not, Mrs Payne. But he's alive.'

She couldn't tell if it was sweat, tap water or tears that flooded Cargill's eyes.

'What happened?'

'We found Luther,' he said. 'He was with his wife, Tarragh. He…,' The words caught as he fought the tremor in his jaw. 'He'd slit his wrists, sitting next to her. It looks as though he bled to death. I don't think there was a drop of blood left in him.'

'But, I thought Tarragh…'

'Mummified. Dead for years. He knew where she was, all that time.'

Laura leant against the wall, her hand over her mouth.

'Please, not in the cellar?'

'Through it. There's a cave.'

'Jesus.'

'There will be body bags,' he said. 'I didn't want you to think it was J.P. Also, we haven't found his brother, Frank. We need specialist help.'

'Could he have got out?'

'Nobody got out.'

He handed the glass back and returned to the incident.

Driving into Milton on the morning that marked five days of living in their new home, two days after the explosion of Luther's, Laura noticed that the waterwheel was turning again.

She parked outside Cargill's office. Through the plate window she saw him jump up. He had the door open before she was out of the truck, biting his bottom lip.

'Mrs Payne, please come in. Hello, Molly.'

Once inside, facing him across his desk as she explained to him how their bedrooms came to be out of commission and would be until the fire damage had been repaired, she observed him relax. Not a slumping back in his executive chair relaxed; more a gradual flattening of the frown, worrying his wedding ring less and a change of focus from her lips to her eyes.

'To which end I am here to contract you to re-employ the same firm, on my behalf.'

'I'd be happy to,' he said leaning forward, offering her his hand, 'no charge. I'm just relieved that it's not more bad news.'

'Why?'

The bluntness of the question punched him back into his chair. It was clear that his guilt didn't sit well on his shoulders.

'You could argue that I brought this down on you.'

'I could,' she said and let it hang in the air for a moment. 'Truth is: we should have looked harder. It was so beautiful – what could possibly go wrong?'

'Well,' he said, attempting a smile that would display his relief, 'it's to be admired that you're both able to see it that way.'

'I don't speak for John.'

He lost the smile.

'The biggest mistake of my life,' he said, 'just to sell a little land.'

'It was business; which is ruthless. It doesn't bring out the best in people.'

Cargill sighed.

'Doesn't have to bring out the worst though, does it?'

'No,' she said, 'I'll grant you that.'

Cargill opened the drawer in his desk and withdrew an envelope.

'This is what he wanted me to give to you.'

'Me?'

'Well, both of you.'

'Let's wait then.'

Cargill opened the drawer in his desk and replaced the envelope. He scratched his chin and looked unsure as to what to do or say next. The silence stretched. For the first time Laura was unable to look at him directly. She played with the lace frill on Molly's sock. She felt Cargill lean forward, adjusting the tone of his voice as though he had guessed what she was about to ask.

'Is there any other way I could be of service, Mrs Payne?'

Laura nodded.

'Would you take me?' she said, lifting her head to look him in the eye.

He took his hand from his face, resting his forearms on the blotter, fingers intertwined.

'It's not a place I'd like to go back to. You'd understand.'

'I want to,' she said. 'Would you stop me?'

'Not up to me. Is it still a crime scene?'

'There's no one there today. Does that mean they've left?'

He shrugged.

'Why do you need to see it?'

'I need to understand. It feels like he turned me inside out. I want to see where Luther was. I need to see where John was. It might be the only way I can help him.'

'How is J.P.?' he asked.

'I don't know.'

Dr Ali Shah was waiting when she arrived at the hospital. A nurse waited with him.

'Good morning, Mrs Payne, and how are you today?'

'I'm better, thank you.'

'Good, good. And how is Molly? Would she like to help the nurses?'

Molly put the fingers of one hand into her mouth and looked up to Laura by way of asking. She had become a favourite with the nurses in the few days John had spent in the hospital. She knew where they kept their biscuits and recognised the trundle of the tea trolley, which she helped push the length of the corridor to the residential sun lounge, where the Venetian blinds sliced the sun into acceptable doses. The elderly residents had adopted Molly too. They enjoyed her company and were happy for her to spend time with them, doing jigsaws and listening to stories she didn't understand. When she had spilled a cup of milky tea over herself, they comforted her with a chorus of 'oh dear's and 'never mind's as they had wiped her dress and legs. Molly was more than happy to take the hand of the nurse, who chatted to her as they walked towards the kitchen.

'She is a lovely child,' said Dr Shah.

'Yes, she is.'

'Come, please, let us talk in my room.'

She grabbed the doctor's arm.

'How's John? Is he okay?'

'Still sleeping.' He indicated the chair at the side of his desk. 'Please.'

The sweet box was on Dr Shah's desk. He took one.

'Physically,' he said, 'there is little more than dehydration wrong with Mr Payne. I'm not overly concerned with the cuts and bruises that, though extensive and gruesome, are largely superficial. I have elected not to stitch the tear in Mr Payne's forehead, opting instead for butterflies. We don't want him to spend the rest of his life looking like Frankenstein's monster, do we?'

He popped the sweet into his mouth.

She'd been surprised at this comment but saw no malice in the doctor's manner and she laughed when he winked at her.

'That's something, I suppose. He'll have enough to deal with.'

'His brother, you mean?'

She didn't answer for a few moments and was acutely aware of the attention of Dr Shah. Frank was gone and she didn't care.

'It may help if you share your thoughts,' he said. 'Of course, if it is none of my business.'

'No, it's not that. I don't want to sound hysterical or paranoid, but...' She paused. 'I'm worried, what Luther did to him, how much of him was left down there. That man down the corridor isn't John, not all of him.'

'Not yet.'

'You really think he'll come back?'

'I expect so, yes. True, his outlook may have changed.'

'An understatement, don't you think?' Before he had a chance to answer Laura fired another question. 'Doctor, did you know?'

Ali Shah took his glasses off as he leant back in his chair.

'We said our goodbyes, Mrs Payne. That is all I know. Had I even an inkling of what Mr Grove had in mind, that he meant to involve others, I would have tried to stop it. This, he knew.'

'You could have stopped him?'

'From taking his own life, no. He saw the cancer as just rewards, something he deserved.'

'You can't know that. Not really.'

'I think I can.'

Rising from his chair he crossed to the examination couch and ran the curtain along its runner, into the wall. She saw the box. He took out a package the size of a large book and returned to sit at his desk. He slid the package across to her. The word LAURA was written on the top. Laura looked from the block capitals to the doctor. He shrugged.

'It was here when I came in on Monday. I have a package also, and some jam.'

'What was the package?'

'His journal.'

'What did you find out?'

'He was not a well man.'

'Why did you wait until now?' she said, indicating the package with her name on it.

'There was a lot going on. It was fraught, compared to how things normally are. I watched.'

'Meaning?'

'You were a patient also. I thought it best to observe.' Dr Shah paused, adjusting his glasses. 'I didn't know how you would react, receiving a package from the man who almost killed your husband and in all likelihood, did kill his brother. I thought other relatives may arrive, to provide support.'

'Both his parents are dead. It was just the two of them.'

'And you?'

'They're alive and well, on their way home from a holiday at my brother's, in Italy.'

'Have you told them?'

'They know, yes. I'm expecting them, tomorrow or the day after.'

'That's good.'

'So, this means?' she said, slipping the package in her bag.

'You appear to be coping, better than Mr Payne I would say.'

'That's to be expected, wouldn't you say? After what Luther put him through?'

'Of course,' said Dr Shah. 'He thought his child was dead. He thought he was going to die. The trauma, the shock,' he said, 'will have an effect.'

He thought he was going to die alone, thought Laura, underground, sharing a grave with his tormentor and the remains of a girl who once looked like her.

The room was cool, clean and white. There was still a strong smell of smoke coming from John. Laura left the door ajar and opened the top window an inch. A fitful breeze caused the net curtain to pulse like a jellyfish. She hadn't sat long before John awoke. He pushed himself up and blinked a few times as he looked around the room, reminding himself where he was.

'Sleep well?' she asked.

'Yeah, I think so. Been here long?'

'Few minutes.'

'Where's Molly?'

'She's doing the tea run.'

'Well, I hope she's getting paid.'

'Well, you're certainly sounding more like your usual self.'

She watched him as he scratched his chin, rasping his nails through his whiskers, causing the intravenous drip attached to his arm to swing on its hook.

'You want a cup?'

'Yeah, but, no rush, I'll wait.'

'It's okay, back in a minute.'

When she returned, she was glad to see he'd got himself up into a sitting position and puffed his pillows behind him. Maybe Dr Shah was right and the fear was leaving. He was looking in the mirror, doing a fingertip examination of the split across his forehead. She rolled the mobile tray into position over the bed and put the mug of tea on it. He put the mirror down.

'Thank you.'

'You're welcome.'

'Have they found Frank yet?'

The question almost stalled in his throat and he wasn't looking at her, choosing instead to stare at the surface of his tea which betrayed the faint trembling in his hand.

'They're still searching.'

He nodded to himself, kept his eyes averted.

'They might never,' he said. 'You know that?'

'We'll see.'

'He said it was deep.'

Laura took a slim wrap of tin foil from her hand bag and opened it on the tray. It contained paper-thin slices of Luther's cured ham. Garnet red in their silver setting; gauzy and pomegranate pink when separated and held between John's fingers. He poked a whole slice into his mouth.

'Nice?'

'Mm, it's good.'

'Thought you'd like it.'

He played with another slice of the ham without actually seeing it, absently forming it into a tube, folding it, breaking it in half. He lifted it to his lips but couldn't eat it. She watched him. He looked up.

'I didn't know.'

She didn't respond.

They sat for a while.

Molly was delivered back from her rounds, jingling her wages in her dress pocket. She climbed onto the bed to help John wipe his eyes. They both shared the remaining slivers.

Dr Shah came in and examined John. Sensitive to his emotional state, he said he would like to observe him for one more night, but expected that tomorrow it should be fine for him to go home, start getting back to normal. Laura thought John's hysterical response to the word 'normal' validated the doctor's earlier diagnosis.

Cargill's Jaguar was in the driveway when Laura arrived home. Glancing up, she saw him walking amongst the ruins of what used to be Luther's home, between the two gable ends. A handful of blue and white police tape fluttered as he gestured for her to come up.

The sheet of plywood that had been fitted across the entrance to the cellar as a makeshift door was clean and bright against the remains of the cottage. The steel padlock glinted in its hasp.

'Looks like a coffin lid,' she said.

The comment looked to hit Cargill hard. It was a while before he turned to her.

'Thought we should get it out of the way,' he said, squinting into the sun. 'I'll come down, see you're alright, but I don't want to go back in.'

Laura felt her grip on Molly tighten.

'Okay.'

'You sure you're okay with that?'

'It's locked,' she said.

He jingled a pair of keys in his spare hand.

'It's official. They know we're here.'

'I don't understand.'

'I had to go to the police. I explained to them, you think it will help you understand your husband more, if you see this. It's therapy.' He shrugged. 'Maybe they think you'll need it. I don't know.'

She moved, eclipsing the sun so that her shadow allowed him to open both eyes.

'Thank you,' she said.

'Don't get ahead of yourself,' he said, springing the lock. 'And don't touch anything.'

'It's still a crime scene?'

'Always will be.'

He lifted two lamps and stepped down into the cellar.

It was colder than she had anticipated, and further. Cargill didn't say a word as he led her along the tunnel. Her arms ached from Molly's weight as she followed him and the pool of light that he carried. Only when the right hand wall disappeared and light flooded into the pitch blackness did he turn to her.

'Watch you don't trip here, and the floor's still a bit wet. Mind and stay to the left.'

'Why, what's down there?'

She followed the ropes that were attached to the steel cleats hammered into the ground. They dropped away steeply and were soon out of the range of the lamps.

'Your brother-in-law,' he said. 'Somewhere. They're coming back tomorrow to continue the search.'

'I see.'

Cargill moved on, along the left hand fork, as Laura looked into the depth and smiled. Molly stretched her arm out to where Cargill had stopped and placed a lamp in the floor.

'It's okay,' said Laura, 'I'm coming. No need to leave one.'

'Not wishing to sound like a suspicious native,' said Cargill, as she arrived, 'but this is as far as I go; seems a natural place to stop.' Laura followed as he looked up. Another sheet of plywood formed part of the ceiling.

'That's where the stream came in?'

'That's the hole that stopped the wheel.'

He handed her the other lamp.

'Is this it?'

'Just down that slope. Watch your head, you'll need to duck.'

She looked ahead. Holding her arm out allowed the light to find the slope. She bit her lip; adjusted Molly on her arm.

'What do I do?'

He shrugged his shoulders.

'Suppose you'll know when you get there.'

He pulled a bag of chocolate buttons from his pocket.

'Will she stay with me?' he said.

Standing inside the cave, Laura could smell woodsmoke and whisky. It was smaller than she had expected. She leant on the post in the floor as she raised the light up to the roof, only to snatch her hand away from the dampness when she realised what it was, what it had been used for. A band of bloody gaffer tape was still attached. The floor at its base was still stained. Chalk outlined where his legs had been, showed the direction he had been facing. She looked away and caught the movement within the oval shadow in the ground ahead of her. Realising it was the play of her lamplight on a dip in the rock, she approached what had to be the place they found Luther and Tarragh.

'Jesus.'

She wiped her fingertips on her jeans.

Luther's blood, where it had sunk into small pocks and indentations, was as tacky and thick as setting jam. Otherwise, the purple stain resembled a birthmark, part of the rock bowl. More chalk lines defined their body positions. Drag stains, where they had been lifted out, were smeared across the floor.

She stood there, trying to imagine what happened. She spun around at a scuffling noise behind her. Beyond the post that John had been bound to, the glow from Cargill's lamp grew at the entrance. Molly's feet appeared, then Molly. Laura put her hand out.

'Hello.'

Molly's chocolate-covered hand instinctively went out to her mother, while her eyes tried to follow the erratic glittering of the walls. Laura took this as a lead and she pointed to the mud hand-prints and the outline of a little girl with her mummy. Molly traced the fingers of a child's hand with her own, until her attention was caught by a piece of mirror wedged into a crack in the rock, then a silver button, a tin foil plate folded into a triangle, and myriad other things, all used as decoration. They explored the cave together at eye level, inspecting each shiny find up close, until they arrived back at the entrance. Molly wandered into the centre of the cave, her head craned to the arching ceiling.

'You okay?'

Molly didn't respond.

'Pooky?' said Laura.

Molly shook her head and smiled.

'Christmas,' she said, pointing to the multi-coloured lights.

'Oh Molly,' said Laura. 'Come here.'

Laura swept her up and hugged her tight. The tears in her eyes gave added sparkle as she held the lamp as high as she could, swinging it around in an attempt to activate each and every reflection as Molly's giggle bubbled out of her. They were dizzy and still laughing when Cargill called to them.

'Everything okay in there?'

Laura closed her mouth, suddenly remembering where she was and why she was there. She lowered the light to chalk-lines and blood. Carrying Molly back towards the exit, she buried her face in her and felt the flutter of eyelashes on her neck.

Laura sat down. Molly nestled within her crossed legs and the bonds of her arms as Laura stared at the post and the bloodstained rock.

'Seen enough?'

'Mr Cargill.'

'Yes, Mrs Payne.'

'It's beautiful.'

There was a significant pause before he responded.

'I'm not with you.'

'You only saw the end,' said Laura, 'the ruination.'

'I can still see it.'

'I'm sorry you had to.'

'Don't be.' His voice was closer. Laura turned to see him

hunkered down in the tunnel end, looking at her. 'I'm sorry for what I said; about it being your fault.'

'Maybe you should speak to the guy who sold us the house.'

He returned her smile.

'Touché. Think you'll be able to help him?'

'Yes.'

'You got your understanding then?'

She kissed Molly on the head.

'Got what I need. I think I understand.'

She reached out for Cargill to help her to her feet.

For the third night running, Laura took Molly into the snug with her, where she had pushed the armchair against the sofa to form an L-shaped bed. With John in the hospital she was company and she was close by. They slept head to head at the heel of the L. For much of the previous two nights Laura had lain awake listening to Molly's breathing, trying to reassure herself.

Tonight, Molly had sat next to Laura as she polished off a bottle of milk before crawling into her chair-bed. She lay with her head on her pillow, watching as Laura unpicked the sellotape on her package and unfolded the wrapping. She used the brown paper to catch the ancient bonding of the album as it cracked and crumbled beneath the force of her fingernails. When she opened it, some of the photographs that had come loose or never been mounted slipped and fell out across the sofa and onto the floor.

'O deah, neber mind,' said Molly, already out of bed to gather them together. As she handed them back she noticed the picture of a little girl and held it up, grinning. 'Molly.'

'No,' said Laura as she took the picture, 'another baby, Ishbel.'

'Ishbel.'

'Yes, Ishbel.'

'Beeman.' Molly's finger squidged into another image she thought she recognised.

'Yes.'

Molly grabbed the album and pulled it towards her, craning her neck to see inside.

'Molly, careful.' She let go, giving her mum the big eyes and instant sadness.

'You want to see?'

Laura patted the sofa beside her and Molly climbed up.

'No touching, okay?'

'Okay.'

Loose photographs of young Luther in parade uniform; in khaki shorts somewhere foreign and warm, bent beneath the bonnet of a camouflaged Land Rover; with a group of men on a packed beach that looked Spanish, with straw hats and red skin; reflected in a mirror in the Horseshoe Bar in Glasgow, seemingly deep in thought. There was also an old black and white of a lady who had his features, and folded blue-prints, for the planned extension to the house.

Laura put these aside and picked up the album.

They started at the beginning, working through the chronology of a life.

The first picture showed Luther, alongside a man too old to be his father, in the doorway of his home. The old man looked sad. Luther didn't look happy. Some landscapes were followed by pictures of the room she was sitting in before it became a ruin. Luther was sat between a couple she assumed to be the Macphersons, who appeared slightly older than him, or farm-worn, in what looked to be the same spot she occupied now. There was a glow to the room that suggested an open fire and tinsel looped across the wall. Three consecutive shots featured the same hitch-hiker, a girl who could only be Tarragh, in shorts and a check shirt, her shoulders straightened by the weight of her rucksack. In the first she was emerging from the trees on the track that came from Milton, dwarfed by them even though they were young and the path had not yet overgrown. The second framed her against the sky, mid way to the house. Her shadow was long, her head cocked, her arms on her hips, staring straight at the photographer. The image was saturated with the evening sun. It made the tree tops gleam, flared through her flaxen hair and gilded the air about her. The roll or sleeping bag that lay across the top of her rucksack drooped behind her, the coy tips of angel's wings. In the third she was right there. She had a curl to her top lip and a beer in one hand while she shaded her eyes with the other, looking straight through the lens. Luther's shadow fell against the wall of his house behind her. Laura put them side by side and knew that Luther fell in love with her within these images. Tarragh literally walked into his life from nowhere.

Over the following pages, as Molly drifted to sleep, Laura walked the streets of Milton with Tarragh; attended the community fireworks, where she made a heart in the air with two sparklers; watched the shinty team as rain fell; rowed across the lochan, swam in the lochan and screamed at the camera as she held her rod upright, the silver fish a blur as it swung through the frame. Laura stared down at Milton from the mountain peak she had only explored on Google, as a half-naked Tarragh swung her bra above her head like a football scarf. Tarragh took Laura underground, to cavern camp-fires, where fish was cooked on long sticks held over the flames, where the ceiling glittered and Luther looked content. She even laughed at Laura over her swollen belly with its protruding button.

And then Ishbel arrived: a newborn swaddled in white, held up next to Tarragh's tired and proud face; mottled and howling during an early bath; eyes closed, suckling at the breast; in the arms of Mr Macpherson who seemed to be smelling her head, while Mrs Macpherson wiped mascara from her face; sleeping on Luther's chest as he lay resting along the couch, his broad hand across her shoulders, fingers spread wide; sitting up in the bowl of an Indian rug thrown over a huge tractor sized inner-tube, a cotton hat against the sun; covered in food, laughing, two white teeth in a sea of tomato sauce; standing with her head inside the washing machine while Tarragh waits behind her, arms laden with dirty laundry; next to Luther, feeding a white horse; next to Tarragh, the pair of them holding up muddy hands, behind them the cavern wall, daubed with handprints; on a deck chair of a ferry boat between Luther's arms that gripped the rail, the blue sea below her, the wind knitting their hair together so that all you could see was two chins and it was obvious they were smiling.

Until she got to what must have been the last picture of Ishbel. The picture that hadn't been stuck in, that had fallen from the album; a little girl in dungarees and red Wellington boots, standing on the boardwalk next to a rowing boat, waving in the direction of her home.

She found herself crying for a man she barely knew, a

wife and child she could never meet and a family that wasn't hers.

They shone from every image.

There was no getting old, no decay of the dream: it just stopped.

Thanks to:

Mum, Dad and Beth for the childhood I still value; Jim and Anne for Fridays, babysitting and much more; Bovy and Caroline for friendship, Barra and financial aid; Jeremy for the Glasgow bed and laughter; Jonny for the Edinburgh bed and stumping up for gig tickets; group C for pulling my work apart; Bovy and Jane Patience for reading early versions of 'Luther' and providing valuable feedback; Adrian and Freight for taking a chance; Rodge Glass for editing that didn't hurt; Carole for never sharing any doubts and Kris Kristofferson for 'To Beat the Devil,' played after encounters with those who did.